Pirates:

The Ring Of Hope

by Daryl K. Cobb

To: Clio
ENJOY reading!

10 To 2 Children's Book

Clinton

10 To 2 Children's Books

Time to Read

Library of Congress Control Number: 2011961913
ISBN-13: 978-0615537436

Printed in the USA

This edition first printing, December 2011

Book design by Daryl K. Cobb
Illustrations by Manuela Pentangelo
Illustations copyright © 2011 by Daryl K. Cobb

Also by
Daryl K. Cobb:

Bill the Bat Finds His Way Home

Daniel Dinosaur

Daddy Did I Ever Say? I Love You,
Love You, Every Day

Bill the Bat Loves Halloween

Bill the Bat Baby Sits Bella

Boy on the Hill

Do Pirates Go To School?

Count With Daniel Dinosaur

Henry Hare's Floppy Socks

Barnyard Buddies: Perry Parrot Finds a Purpose

Pirates: Legend of the Snarlyfeet

Greta's Magical Mistake

Mr. Moon

For Daryl's books,
music and author visit information:
www.darylcobb.com

ACKNOWLEDGMENTS

In the process of my writing there is one person who is often overlooked, but it is with her exceptional skills that my words and thoughts are conveyed coherently, spelled correctly and free from grammatical errors. Editing is a talent that is taken for granted and with this book, longer and more detailed than any I have written previously, I want to make sure that my editor gets the recognition she deserves. Not one of my stories has crossed her desk that she hasn't scrutinized and in some way made better. The reader doesn't have to experience the initial mistakes (and yes, I do make a few) -- tenses are used correctly, run-on sentences are slashed and separated, and if something just doesn't make sense, it is sorted through and fixed. On top of all of that, every period, dash and comma is in its proper place when the story leaves her hands.

For all of this, thank you! Thank you for caring that my work is the best that it can be. Thank you for your feedback and for giving me things to think about. It is hard to go into a rewrite without knowing what isn't working and your input has always been appreciated.

In addition to acknowledging the

behind-the-scenes help I received in bringing this book to print, I want to share with my readers that "The Ring of Hope", aside from being a fantastical adventure story, is really about the survival of family. It contains many elements from my own personal experiences and I believe that those are the moments that give the story life. I would not have any of these memories to share, however, if it weren't for the people who have been part of my life's journey. It is those people to whom I dedicate this book:

Joanne, Cameron and Kayley, you are always my inspiration!

Mom and Dad, for instilling in me in childhood, even if I didn't believe it at the time, that family is important.

Shawn, Colin and Erin, you have each grown into someone who I enjoy being with. I am glad that we have all come together.

All of my friends who don't think twice about helping someone in need, thank you for your support.

Manuela Pentangelo, who has been with me from the first book, your talent inspires me daily!

Those I've lost, without whom life is not the same --

   Sal and Chris Salimbeno, the best inlaws a guy could have hoped for, we miss you both so very much.

   Ethel Cobb, my grandmother, whose love and kindness helped shape my life, I hope that I have made you proud.

   Jimmy Melick, whose work ethic was inspiring, you showed me that success takes persistence. You're in my heart.

   Dave Porcelli, who I miss and think of often. Go Phillies.

Table of Contents

Daryl K. Cobb

Pirates: Chapter 1

The Ring

Buried in the sand on the island of Hoganthal was a treasure that would fill every pirate's dreams, or so they thought. This treasure did not include gold challises or doubloons, and there were no diamonds or rubies or emeralds. Buried here was a plain black box, and in this box was a single gold ring with the inscription, "To all who need hope". This ring was known to have special powers and every pirate who heard tales of the ring had it in his mind that it would someday be his. The ring was known by all as The Ring of Hope.

It was said that in the heat of battle this ring would bring one's enemies to their knees and make men disappear before their eyes. But this was as close to the truth as the stories ever got. Through the years the accounts of what this ring could do inflated to include extraordinary feats, some almost biblical in effect, like Moses parting the Red Sea. The true purpose of this ring, however, was really only known to those who had worn it, and even they didn't know its full abilities. But to those who sought it, it meant power, and power meant riches. So the perceived value of this simple gold ring was enormous.

What people didn't know about the ring was that it had limited powers and, most importantly, it could not be worn by just anyone. The Ring of Hope would only bond with the heart and soul of a man of its choosing -- someone it deemed worthy -- and the wearer of the ring had to stay true to the ring's intent or face the same consequences as those who the ring failed to choose. The ring was created with one goal in mind, and that was to preserve mankind at its best as the rest of humanity tried to destroyed itself.

The Ring of Hope was named because of its ability to give the wearer an out -- if you were in a situation that was dire and there was no hope of escape, the energy from this ring would transport you to safety. In the eyes of your enemy you would just vanish, and this is how the ring became a legend. But there were many problems for those who claimed ownership of this gold band, and all of them were brought on by the legend itself.

Every pirate reveled in the thought of being invincible, so pirates came looking for this ring in droves. The families of the bearers of the ring would soon become targets. Some would be taken and used as leverage to get the owner to hand over the ring, and some, though it was rare, would become casualties in a struggle to keep it. In order to protect their families, most of the ring's owners would leave their homes and live like fugitives from the law, always running and hiding. For a piece of gold that was supposed to bring hope, it mostly created situations that often seemed hopeless, and, because of this, the ring would be cast away by its owners. But getting rid of the ring didn't stop the pirates from thinking that it was just being hidden, so most owners came to regret that decision. In their minds they thought that without the ring they could return to a normal life. Unfortunately, once you had the ring, it was impossible to return to what used to be, yet without the ring, there was no chance to escape the virtual lawlessness of the times. The ability to be free and happy was all within the ring's power to give, but the owner had to have the faith to become one with the ring. The ring's deepest powers were seldom discovered and, because of this, the wearer would loose faith in it. That was the case with Emmit Whalbash.

When Emmit Whalbash, the last known owner of the ring, slipped the gold band off his finger for the final time, he took a deep breath and, without the slightest bit of hesitation, he dropped it into a small black box and shut the lid. As he dug the hole that would soon become the final resting place for his box he thought of his family and how much he missed them. Emmit wanted his life back the way it used to be. He wanted to wake up next to his wife and not be afraid; he wanted to know that his children had a chance to live normal lives; and, what Emmit wanted most was for this ring to be gone forever. It was his intent to make sure that this box was never found, that this ring would never be worn again by anyone, and that is how The Ring of Hope found its way beneath the white sand beaches of Hoganthal. Emmit tossed the last shovel full of sand onto the top of the pile that now filled the hole. He stood still for a moment, like a mourner paying his last respects, then climbed back into his boat and sailed back out to sea.

For years people searched for Emmit and his ring but neither was ever found. Rumors spread that Emmit and the ring were both taken by the sea. Eventually the pirates lost interest and moved on to finding more tangible riches. Hoganthal was just an island in passing; that was, until people started to discover the riches of its natural resources.

Hoganthal was home to hundreds of different species of animals, some that brought great prices. It also had an abundance of tropical plants and fruits and, to the dismay

4

of some travelers, it soon became a popular place for the King's Navy to take anchor. Groups of men would go to shore each day and spend hours exploring the island while one sailor stayed behind to keep watch on their boat. One very hot summer day, Navy Seaman Ardin J. Delham had the honor of standing watch.

The Ring of Hope had stayed hidden in the sand for nearly one hundred years when Seaman Delham stumbled over a turtle's nest while taking a look around the beach. Ardin landed on the spot where it had been buried and his hand went just deep enough into the sand for him to feel the lid of Emmit's box. Out of simple curiosity, Ardin decided to brush the sand away. To his surprise, he discovered the unmistakenly old black box, and inside the box was one small gold ring that looked like a man's wedding band. It was so common looking that he couldn't understand why anyone would go through the trouble of burying it, until he saw the inscription, "To all that need hope". One hundred years of waves beating down on the beach, along with many violent volcanic eruptions, were just enough to inch Emmit's box slowly to the surface, until it was close enough to finally be touched.

When Ardin read the inscription his eyes grew wide -- he knew instantly what he was holding. This ring was a legend that transcended many generations and the stories that surrounded it, both good and bad, came to mind.

Was he now holding it? And was it now his? Ardin carefully slipped the ring onto his finger and, when it had slid into place, he didn't know what to think. Somehow he thought he would feel different, that maybe something magical would happen, but there was nothing. He didn't feel stronger or invincible. He didn't feel smarter. He was exactly the same. He couldn't help but think that all the stories behind this ring must have been lies, but one thing he knew for certain was that it was now his and, no matter what, he would not tell anyone what he had found. It would be his secret and, with this thought in his head, he walked to the edge of the jungle beyond the beach and tossed the black box away.

Ardin went on to live a happy and full life. He left the King's Navy after five years of service and stayed on in the new world where he had met a beautiful young woman by the name of Elizabeth Eldersby. Ardin and Elizabeth fell in love and were married. They went on to have two handsome sons, Charles and Paul. For forty years, Ardin wore The Ring of Hope and was lucky enough to have never needed its powers. At the end of his life he would take comfort in knowing that his family gave him all the hope he had ever needed. His wife and sons never knew where this ring had come from and, when Ardin died at age sixty-three, his sons saw it only as a memento of their father. Even though both boys would have liked to have had the ring, custom was that it

6

would go to Charles as the eldest. So, upon Ardin's death, the ring was removed from his finger and placed into a blue velvet box along with a personal note that Ardin had written years before.

The period after Ardin's death was a painful time for both brothers. While Paul missed his father deeply and clung onto the memories that made him the happiest, of which there were many, Charles held onto anger and resentment. Ardin loved both of his boys equally, but to Charles, Paul was always the favorite. Now that his father was gone, Charles would never be able to make him see that Paul was nothing special and that it was Charles who was really the special child. For Charles, this pain would not go away. Ardin's death left a hole in both boys' lives that no amount of money could fill, but in Charles's mind, when all was said and done, he came up the loser again.

Elizabeth had been thinking about Charles and about Ardin's ring for days after Ardin's death and she was struggling with carrying out his instructions. To Elizabeth's knowledge she was the only person besides Ardin who had ever seen the inscription on his ring and, even though he had never told her where it came from, she knew of the legend and had surmised years ago that this could be The Ring of Hope. She loved Charles very much but for years she could see her son's anger and hostility growing. She didn't know where it came from, but it was there. First it was directed at Ardin, and it seemed like it was just part of his growing up, turning from a boy into a man. But as the years went on, she knew it was much deeper than that. As Elizabeth watched her sons interact over the seven days since Ardin's passing, she cringed at how Charles treated Paul. He had turned into a very cold man and she couldn't help but wonder what was going on inside his head, and fear that it was only going to get worse. Based on this fear, Elizabeth made a decision, and even though Ardin might not like what she was about to do, she knew he would have understood. Charles was the wrong choice for taking ownership of the ring.

Elizabeth called both of her sons into her husband's study. When they walked in she was standing behind his large walnut desk, and on the top of the desk sat two small blue velvet boxes. In each box was a gold band -- one was the ring that came from Ardin and the second was a duplicate. It was Elizabeth's hope that this gesture would be enough to set Charles's mind at ease.

"Come in, sit down," said Elizabeth. "Your father and I talked about his estate in great length before his passing and we both felt that he had done a good job of splitting it up fairly between the two of you. However, one thing was left out of the estate, a piece of jewelry that your father was very fond of. I know you both know what I am talking about."

8

"Yes, Mother, the ring," said Charles, smiling.

"Yes, the ring," Elizabeth replied. "I knew that this ring would have significant meaning to both of you because your father loved it so. But there are two sons and only one ring."

"Mother, Charles is the eldest and I have already prepared myself for the ring to be passed to him," Paul said.

Charles had been waiting for this day since Ardin's death. He wanted that ring and was ready to fight for it so he was a little surprised, and even a little disappointed, that Paul let it go so easily.

"That won't be necessary, Paul. I took several pieces of your father's favorite gold jewelry and, together with the gold band, had them melted down and made into two identical rings." Elizabeth picked up the boxes and leaned forward, handing one to each son. "I thought that it was important for both of you to have his ring. This way, you each have part of it. Please open your boxes and try them on so I know that they are sized correctly."

Paul opened his first and, with a big grin on his face, slipped it on his finger.

"Mother, it fits perfectly! Thank you so much. This means a lot to me." Paul stood up and walked over to his mother and kissed her on the cheek.

"You're welcome, Darling. I am so glad that you like it. Charles, my dear, put yours on."

"Charles, put it on," said Paul cheerfully. "Put it on."

"No, I will not!" Charles responded like an angry child. "Mother, you destroyed father's ring! How could you do that? He loved that ring."

"Charles, now listen . . ." Elizabeth tried to explain, but Charles cut her off, yelling,

"It should have been mine! Not a piece of it -- the whole thing. I was the first born and it was my right."

Elizabeth was stunned. She was being scolded like a child by her own son! She was hurt and extremely embarrassed. His disrespect was reprehensible and she would not stand for it.

"Your right?" Elizabeth screamed in anger. "How dare you talk to me like that! As your father's wife, that ring belongs to *me*. I will choose to give it to whom I want and it was my decision that it would be shared. If you don't like it then don't wear it. But don't you ever talk to me like that again, do you understand me?" Elizabeth, visibly shaking, eased herself down into a chair.

"Fine, but I will not wear that ring," Charles said pointedly. He slammed the unopened box on the desk and walked out of the room, leaving Paul and Elizabeth in shock.

"Mother, I am so sorry," said Paul.

"It is not your fault, it is mine. In a way, your brother is right. It should have been his."

"Then why didn't you just give him the ring? I would have been fine with that."

"But I wouldn't have," said Elizabeth sadly.

"Mother, why? It's just a ring."

"It's not *just* a ring, Paul. Remove it for a second. I want you to see something."

Paul eased the band off of his finger. "What do you want me to see?"

"On the inside of your ring is an inscription. Can you read it?"

"Yes, 'To all that need hope'."

"Have you ever heard stories about The Ring of Hope?"

"Yes, of course I have. That is the inscription that is said to be on it."

"Yes, it is," said Elizabeth softly.

"Why would you have it engraved on my ring?"

"I didn't, Paul. It was already on the ring."

"How is that possible, Mother? You said you just had these made?"

"I wasn't telling the truth, Paul. That ring is your father's ring. I didn't melt it down to divide it, I just had a second ring made for Charles."

Paul stood silent for a second trying to absorb what he just heard. "If this is my father's ring, Mother, this ring should have been given to Charles. He is the first born. Is this what father wanted?"

"It is what I wanted and I now believe that your father would agree with my decision."

"But he wanted Charles to have the ring?"

"Yes, he did."

"Then why would you go against his wishes?"

Elizabeth rose from her chair and stood directly in front of her son. Paul now towered over her but, at five feet seven, she was a tall woman, tall enough to reach up and take Paul's face gently between her hands. She spoke to Paul in almost a whisper, "Because you have a kind heart and I know that you can handle the power and responsibility that come with this ring. Your brother cannot, and I am now certain that your father would agree."

"But how do you know this is really the The Ring of Hope? Father told you this?"

"No, I don't know for sure that it is, but the inscription for me is telling, and I am confident enough in my belief that I would wager everything I have on it. Your father kept this ring a secret from everyone, including me, and he had to have had his reasons. I think whatever his reasons were must mean something. Your father was a smart man and, if this is The Ring of Hope, I think being secretive was a wise choice, don't you?"

"Yes, Mother, a very wise choice."

"Good. Now put it back on your finger, for it is now yours, and let me make us some lunch."

Paul wanted to be happy with his mother's decision, but deep in his heart he couldn't help but feel bad for Charles. The ring, whether it was or wasn't The Ring of Hope, should have been given to him. Paul slid the ring back on his finger and watched it fall perfectly into place. It looked good on his hand and Paul felt a rush of happiness, like his father had just given him a pat on the back. The Ring of Hope also felt right at home on Paul's hand, just like it had for Ardin when he found it.

13

Pirates: Chapter 2

The Dilemma

Catherine turned the last page of Peter's story and found herself hoping that there was more to come but, to her disappointment, there was not. She stacked the pages back together, took a deep breath and exhaled. She shook her head in frustration, picked up her pen and scribbled a note at the top of the title page. Next to the note she wrote "A-" and then she moved on to the next paper. After reading three more stories that she marked confidently with C pluses, her thoughts returned to the A minus. Catherine had read Peter's story twice and she was having an ethical dilemma. The paper deserved an A plus and she knew it. The story was written by one of her favorite students and it was everything a teacher could hope for out of a writing assignment. But the story was, once again, about pirates!

Peter was a gentle, creative soul with a wild imagination and by far one of her best writers. For some reason, however, he had a strange infatuation with pirates and had a knack for turning every writing assignment into a pirate story. It was driving Catherine nuts. She just wanted him to write about things that kids do -- be a kid, she would tell him, and write about things you can relate to. Incorporate everyday experiences, like hanging with your friends, playing video games and sports, so that your reader feels a connection. But, instead, Peter's stories had him sword fighting with bands of renegade pirates, fishing for great white sharks off of the Ivory Coast or hunting for treasure on islands infested with dragons. So, yes, even though she knew that this story deserved an A plus, she was reluctant to encourage him to continue down this path. She wanted him to grow and expand his writing so she couldn't help but think that by giving his paper the grade it deserved that she was, in fact, encouraging him. Catherine knew if the story was written by anyone other than Peter it would have warranted an A plus. She really didn't know what do with him.

Catherine liked Peter very much. He was always well behaved in class and very respectful. In her opinion, this was the result of good parenting, but lately she had started to wonder if something might be going on at home; if something in his once stable environment had changed. He didn't seem quite himself as of late and the pirate infatuation was starting to border on obsession. She knew that many behavioral changes in students Peter's age were the result of problems in the students' home lives, like parents splitting up or losing a close relative, but it could be anything, from lack of sleep and depression to dating problems or just plain insecurity.

She thought about the idea of Peter dating and it made her smile. Catherine loved observing the students who were "dating" in school. It just amused her to no end. They would simply walk side by side down the hallway -- no hand holding, no arms wrapped around waists or shoulders. For most of the kids at this age, dating was little more than the exchange of phone calls, e-mails and text messages, with a few of the more daring boys and girls going so far as to see a movie together or go home on the bus to one of their houses after school. They were at an age where they had already discovered that cooties didn't exist and that boys and girls could enjoy each other's company, but watching them struggle with the adult concept of dating and trying to apply it to their world was interesting. However, in trying to figure out what could be happening in Peter's personal life to affect his behavior, girl issues would not have been on the top of Catherine's list. She had not noticed Peter spending a lot of time with any one girl during school hours so she dismissed this as the cause of Peter's recent change. But she couldn't rule out that insecurity in general might be starting to sneak up on him.

Peter's appearance had changed a lot over the summer break with his height and hair being the most obvious. Catherine was only guessing, but he had to have shot up nearly six inches in the two and a half months since the end of the previous school year. At five foot seven he was starting to look like a boy in a man's body which made her think that he could be feeling a little insecure. Then there was his hair; it had gotten so long that even she had mistaken him for a girl a few times when he had been seated and she had seen him from behind. She had to admit that he did have great hair, feeling even a hint of jealousy of the perfect waves and how it shined in the light. Catherine had even heard other female teachers comment on how no boy should be blessed with such gorgeous hair and she agreed it just wasn't fair.

What concerned Catherine about Peter the most, though, was the fact that he was starting to really stand out from the crowd and, at twelve and thirteen years old, being different from everyone could result in being shunned and alienated by your peers. She noticed this starting to happen in small ways, like some boys teased him about his hair. The comments right now seemed to be all in fun but, as time goes on, kids can tend to get meaner and others may start to join in because they see their friends doing it. As a middle school teacher, Catherine had seen it happen many times through the years and she didn't want to see it happen to Peter. It was at that moment that she decided two important things: one was that she was going to talk to him and see if she could get him to open up about what might be bothering him, and the second was that the A minus had to stay. She knew that the best of Peter's writing was yet to come and she was going to find a way to pull it out of him.

The bell rang, startling Catherine out of her preoccupied state of mind. She straightened out the pile of graded papers and collected her thoughts for her incoming class. She was happy it was the last class of the day; happier still that she might get that opportunity to talk to Peter afterwards and see if she could get him to provide at least a hint as to what was going on with him. As the students started to fill the classroom, Catherine smiled, walked up to the chalkboard and starting to write down the key points of the day's lesson.

*   *   *

"Finally, before we end for the day, I want to tell everyone what a wonderful job you've done with the first chapter of your stories. I enjoyed reading all of them, but now I want all of you to bring more of yourselves

18

into your stories. The assignment for Monday is for you to pick something that happened to you this week and write about it. Next week we will read them in class and talk about how you can tie those personal experiences into your stories. Again, this is due on Monday. Write that in your agendas so you don't forget. Also, on your way out, stop at my desk and pick up your stories, and Peter, if you could stay for just one minute, there's something I'd like to talk to you about. Everyone have a great weekend," Catherine said as the bell rang.

Peter stayed seated as the rest of the students hurried out of the classroom. He couldn't imagine what he had done to be asked to stay after class -- his homework was always on time and he had gotten A's on almost every paper so far this marking period. As the last student exited the classroom Catherine grabbed a chair and seated herself next to Peter's desk.

"Peter," said Catherine, "I want to ask you something."

"Did I do something wrong, Miss Wells?"

"Oh, no, Peter, you didn't do anything wrong. I'm just concerned, that's all."

"About what?"

"About you. You just don't seem like your usual happy self lately."

Peter looked down at the floor. "Sorry."

"Peter, you don't have to apologize. I thought you

19

seemed very distracted in class this week and I just want to see if there is anything wrong."

Peter just looked at Catherine. He wasn't really sure what he should say next, so he didn't respond.

"Is there anything you want to talk about?" Catherine encouraged.

"No, not really."

"Does 'not really' mean there *is* something but you don't want to talk about it?"

"It's nothing," said Peter.

"It's nothing," repeated Catherine. "That means that there is something? Peter, if someone at school is bothering you or hurting you, please tell me," Catherine said with a look of concern.

"No, that's not it."

"Then what is it, Peter?" Catherine could see that it was on the tip of his tongue.

"It's Monk," he said.

"Monk?" Catherine looked confused. "The Monk from your stories?"

"Yes," said Peter.

Monk was a reoccurring character in Peter's stories but Catherine hadn't realized that he was real so she was surprised. "So this whole week you've been worried about your pet?" she asked.

"Yes."

"And what happened to Monk that has you all

20

worried?"

"He left the house on Monday and I haven't seen him since."

"Oh, Peter, I am so sorry to hear that, but I'm sure he will come home. For all you know, he came back while you were in school today."

"I hope so."

"And that's it, there is nothing else?"

"Nope."

"Well, let's hope he comes home soon because I need the old you back in class," Catherine said jokingly.

"He will," said Peter, "I know that. I just didn't think he'd be gone this long."

Catherine smiled and was relieved that it wasn't anything more serious. "Peter, there is one more thing."

Peter looked concerned again.

"This has to do with your school work and this weekend's writing assignment. You are one of my best writers and I love reading about your pirate adventures, but this assignment is strictly personal. You must write about what is really happening in your life."

"I thought that's what I was doing."

"I am not seeing it, Peter. You are writing fantasy, and even though I can see that you are trying to make it personal, it is still missing the basis in reality that I have been stressing in class. I believe that once you figure out how to take things from your real life and use them in

21

your writing you will make that personal connection with your reader that will pull them in completely. Treasure hunts and sea adventures are exciting, Peter, but I want you to reach in your heart and tell me a story about Peter Nichols. Can you do that for me?" Catherine almost pleaded.

"I think so," Peter replied, trying not to sound puzzled even though he was.

"Good! I hope a lot of fun things happen this weekend for you to write about, and I'll look forward to reading about them on Monday. Have a good weekend, Peter," Catherine said cheerfully. She stood up, and Peter did the same. "And Peter?"

"Yes, Miss Wells?"

"I hope Monk comes home soon."

Peter smiled and said, "Thank you, me too."

Peter walked out of class and into the weekend. He thought about what Miss Wells had said and wondered how he could connect his pirate world to the present times in a way that would make her see that he *was* truly connected to what he was writing about. To her, he was writing about fantasies but, to Peter, it was his world. His world included sailing the sea, treasure hunts, pirates and Monk. Peter would write about his life this weekend, as he had promised his teacher, but first he needed to see if Monk had returned home.

Back in the classroom, Catherine looked down at her

desk and noticed that Peter forgot to take his story home. She picked it up and started to put it in her desk drawer but then she stopped. Catherine looked at the clock on the wall, smiled, then sat down in her chair and started reading it again.

Pirates: Chapter 3

The Job Offer

First Mate Pantuzzo let Antonio into the captain's quarters and told him to have a seat at the map table. Then he walked away, letting the door shut behind him. The table was large enough to seat six men but it only had seating for four. It was a dark mahogany wood, polished so it glimmered in the light, and had matching chairs. Antonio was not a sizable man -- he possibly topped at one hundred and sixty pounds after a hearty dinner and he stood only five feet five, easily the shortest man in his circle of friends -- so he sat in the last seat facing the door to have a good view of anyone entering the room. He never liked to be caught off guard. The chair he sat in was so large that it seemed to swallow him up. He looked like a child sitting there instead of the formidable foe that he was.

Most people who hired Antonio did so because they knew that they could count on him to get the job done in a way that left no tracks. Antonio was quick on his feet, agile and a good fighter, and he wasn't afraid to get his hands dirty, but he did try to avoid confrontation when possible. He was a dangerous man when he needed to be and his slight frame fooled most adversaries into letting down their guard, which often made the difference between life and death. Antonio had a gregarious personality and a knack for talking his way out of trouble -- in a worst case scenario he could at least control the situation until the moment presented itself to strike. Darfous Warner was rumored to share a similar reputation so when Antonio was presented with the possibility of working for him, he was fascinated.

This being Antonio's first time in a captain's quarters, he was looking around the room, taking it all in, and he decided that it wasn't bad at all. A little too upper crust for his taste, but nice. There was a hint of lavender in the air, even though Antonio didn't see any flowers to go with the scent. It was a far cry from the crew's quarters that he had slept in years ago that offended with a mix of identifiable smells, ranging from pungent feet to body odor to the unmistakable stink of pirates passing gas as a direct result of the ship's bad food. The room could have been a little larger, but it was comfortable and the furnishings fit perfectly. There was a desk that was an exact match in color to the map table he was sitting at, and it was meticulously cluttered with logbooks, other work papers and the captain's personal belongings.

Antonio was trying to get an idea of what Warner was like by examining his possessions. On the desk he saw a quill and some parchment but, without changing his position or standing, he couldn't make out everything on the desk. There was a door, presumably the entrance to the captain's bedroom, on one wall and against another was a lone black leather chair with an end table placed next to it and an oil lamp on top of that. Antonio assumed this was where the captain did his pleasure reading and wished that he could try the chair out for himself. Above the chair was a painting of a ship engaged in battle with its canons firing. The painting caught and held Antonio's attention for a while as it was an exact likeness of the Fighting Skull. The Skull, as it was notoriously known, was one of the biggest pirate ships ever built and it was a beauty (unless, of course, it was coming at you with guns blazing). The Fighting Skull belonged to Captain Darfous Warner and Antonio couldn't help but wonder if the man behind the infamous ship would be as imposing and intimidating as the ship itself.

Pantuzzo popped back through the door, startling Antonio, and said, "The captain will be right in." He left as quickly as he entered and, moments later, he reentered behind Captain Darfous Warner.

Warner was an older man, probably in his late sixties, and about eight inches taller than Antonio. He almost had to duck down to walk through the doorway into the cabin. The captain wore a white wig and spectacles, looking somewhat more dignified than your typical pirate. Despite the grandiose stories that circulated about Warner's fierce nature and impressive conquests, when Antonio saw him he saw a tired old man and couldn't help but think that his time had come and gone. Warner appeared to be almost grandfatherly in nature, but Antonio knew that was an act that had simply been mastered over time. Pantuzzo stood at the door like a watchman holding two leather pouches and a box big enough to store a pair of women's shoes. Antonio stood up to greet the captain.

"Be seated, Mr. Trovol," the captain said.

"Yes, sir," said Antonio.

"I have friends in high places and they tell me that you are a trustworthy sort. Would they be correct?"

"Yes, sir."

"They also tell me you are tight-lipped and that you do what you are told without question. Is that also true?"

"Yes, sir."

"Good. That is the type of man I am looking for. I

have a few jobs that could put a substantial amount of money in your pockets. Are you interested?"

"I'm listening."

"Good!" said Warner, sounding excited. " Since we have never worked together before, I am going to start by giving you one very easy task to complete. If you do this task successfully, you and I are going to become very good friends."

"What is it you want me to do?" Antonio asked.

"Not so fast, Mr. Trovol. I think we need to be clear on a few things before we get to the job."

"Like what?"

"Mistakes, for instance. I won't tolerate them. I absolutely will not listen to excuses and failure is not an option. I probably don't need to tell you that but I want to make everything clear from the start."

"It's clear and, by the way, I don't ever fail."

"I have heard that about you, so I didn't think you would. If I thought otherwise, you wouldn't be sitting here. Mr. Pantuzzo, will you approach." Pantuzzo approached the table and tossed down the two thick leather pouches which slid to a stop right in front of Antonio. "Mr. Trovol, all I want you to do is to deliver a package."

"You are going to pay me to deliver a package?"

"It is a special gift and I need a man who I can trust to deliver it. Can I trust you?"

"Of course you can," said Antonio.

Warner listened carefully to how Antonio answered his question and didn't detect the slightest bit of hesitation in his response. The captain paused a second longer and then proceeded. "Mr. Trovol, in front of you is all the information you'll need to carry out what I want done, and your wage is being paid in advance. Flip open the top folder and you will see."

Antonio opened the folder and his eyes grew very large as he let his thumbs flip through the bills.

Warner continued, "It's a lot of money for such an easy task, I know, and much more than you deserve, but I like to keep my men happy. But for this amount of money I have a few requirements and you must abide by them if you decide to accept. First, it is important that you complete this task within the next two weeks. Not a minute over. And second, under no circumstances are you to tell anyone that you are working for me. This assignment requires complete secrecy -- you can not tell a soul. Do I make myself clear?"

"Yes, sir. I can't tell anyone." Antonio was getting a little tired of being talked to like he was a child, but he tried his best not to show it.

"If by chance the cat gets out of the bag or you are seen or, worse, caught in the act, you will be released from my services. As a matter of fact, I will deny ever knowing you and I will also expect all monies to be returned. Not to mention I will have Mr. Pantuzzo feed you to the sharks." Captain Warner looked at Antonio and started to laugh. "I am only kidding, Antonio," he chuckled.

But Antonio knew he was dead serious.

"I can call you Antonio, yes?" asked the captain.

"Yes, sir. I would prefer that you did."

"How do you feel about these terms, Antonio?"

"I am fine with them, Captain."

"Okay then, the job is yours, which is good for me because I couldn't get anyone else to agree to them." The captain started laughing again but, again, Antonio knew he was probably telling the truth.

"That leaves one more thing -- you will need a helper. I don't care who you choose but I would prefer that you don't use a friend. Emotions get the best of us when we have to make tough choices, do you understand me?"

"Yes, sir, I do."

"Good. Well, I think this meeting is concluded."

"Excuse me, Captain," interjected Pantuzzo. He had been so quiet throughout the meeting that Antonio had forgotten he was in the room.

"Yes, Mr. Pantuzzo."

"You forgot this, sir," Pantuzzo said, holding up the box.

"Where is my head! Antonio, the box is your assign-ment. You must deliver this. Give him the box already

-- thank you, Mr. Pantuzzo. Now, Antonio, I would like to give you a little warning about this box. You will open it and when you do you will see a bottle with a note inside it. You will think to yourself, 'I would like to read what is written on that note,' and I want to tell you, man to man, that if you do you will die. It may take some time, but it will be painful and you will die. Am I clear?"

"Yes, sir, perfectly clear."

"With that being said, I think we are done. It was a pleasure meeting you," Warner concluded with the warmest of smiles.

"Yes, sir, a pleasure," Antonio said, not meaning it in the least.

Antonio slid his chair out from the table and stood. He tucked the box under his arm, picked up the two leather pouches and started to follow Pantuzzo to the door.

"Stop, stop, stop!" Captain Warner said suddenly. Antonio almost jumped out of his skin. "I can't believe this slipped my mind! Antonio, do you know what a Carma Monkey is?"

"No, sir, I don't."

"Well then, come with me. I am going to introduce you to one of the most interesting animals in the world."

Captain Warner walked out of his quarters with Antonio and Pantuzzo following closely behind. Sailors filled the ship's deck doing their various chores and

31

Antonio knew it was a life he did not want to return to at forty-four years of age. A sailor's life required way too much physical work with little appreciation from anyone for your efforts. He preferred being the mystery bad guy, the guy who solved people's problems. He found it enjoyable.

Antonio's line of work was not for the faint of heart, but he found excitement in it. He almost felt like a spy. He was hired to sneak silently into places that he was not supposed to be and acquire things. Okay, maybe it was stealing, and stealing is wrong, but he *is* a pirate and that is what pirates do.

Antonio was good at what he did so the work was plentiful. Being the best at something gave Antonio the comfort of being able to pick and choose his jobs and he was at a point where he turned down more than he accepted. He was very cautious, and he would not take any assignment that required physical confrontation. It wasn't that he couldn't handle himself, but it was a moral issue for Antonio -- he did not want to be responsible for altering the course of someone's future or, more likely in his line of work, causing an end to it.

Unfortunately, there was that occasional situation where confrontation was just unavoidable and it could not be resolved without someone getting hurt. When this happened, it would weigh heavily on Antonio's heart and he always remembered what his mom would say --

confession is good for the soul. So, after a night that didn't go well, Antonio would go to church the next morning and sit through mass, sometimes even two if it had been a really bad night. But even after a good mass there was always something nagging at him, and he knew the only way to put his mind at ease would be to go confession.

"Bless me, Father, for I have sinned. My last confession was yesterday. Father, I am not sure how to say this, but let's just say I hurt a man. It wasn't part of my original plan, but the man happened to be in the wrong place at the wrong time and he saw me."

"You need to make peace with God and try to control your temper, my son," the priest would reply.

"Yes, Father, I will try."

"Do you have anything else to confess?"

"Yes, Father. I have stolen and I feel awful, but the man I hurt had things on him that I knew he wouldn't need once we had concluded our business so I took them."

"My son, you need to make peace with God and maybe you should think about finding this man and returning what you took."

"Yes, Father, I would really like to do that."

"Good. Is there anything else?"

"Yes, Father, I lied. I told this man that I wouldn't hurt him and I did anyway."

"Your anger seems to be a continuing problem. You have to learn to control it. You also must make amends with this man."

"Yes, Father, I will do that. Do you think sending flowers is appropriate?"

"It sounds like a start, my son."

Antonio had found a way to make peace with what he did for a living and, as he followed the captain across the deck and watched the men work, his prior thinking that he never wanted to work that hard again was reaffirmed. At the other end of the deck, the captain walked through a door into the crew's sleeping quarters. Antonio and Pantuzzo followed him in.

"Now this is what I remember," Antonio said under his breath as he gazed around the room. The sleeping quarters for the crew was cramped, dirty and smelled exactly how it looked. As they walked through the bunks, the assault on Antonio's senses gave him yet further confirmation that this type of life was not for him.

Warner kept walking until he came to a second door at the far end of the room. He pushed the door open and stepped inside. With a wave of his hand, Warner motioned for Antonio to follow him, but this time Pantuzzo remained at the door to stand watch. The moment Antonio stepped fully into the room his brow furrowed and his jaw dropped slightly. Sitting on a chair in front of them, in the center of the room, was the cutest monkey

34

he had ever seen. It was also the most unusual monkey he had ever seen -- blue, and furry like a panda.

"Antonio, I would like to introduce you to Stella. She is my baby," the captain declared proudly. Warner rubbed the monkey's head and she seemed truly excited to see him. "Stella does lots of tricks, don't you Stella?"

Stella nodded her head and smiled.

"Now, Antonio, I will apologize right now if she gets this wrong, but keep in mind that I just started teaching it to her yesterday. Are you ready, Stella?" Again Stella nodded her head. "Okay then," said Warner, "I want you to show our guest what I taught you."

Antonio was amused and almost started to laugh. He could just imagine this old man sitting around playing with his monkey and he found this funny. This was an affirmation of his first thought when he saw Warner walk into the captain's quarters, that this man's time had definitely come and gone.

"Come on, Stella, don't be shy," encouraged the captain.

Stella leapt off of the chair she was sitting on and made her way over to Antonio. Antonio thought again that she was very cute, and then Stella grabbed hold of his pants leg and climbed up his body. She stopped when she could grasp onto his shoulder. Antonio's body became tense and he began to tremble a bit from anxiety.

The captain must have sensed his uneasiness and said, "Relax, Antonio. Stella will not hurt you." Then, turning his attention back to the monkey, he said, "Okay, Stella, you are doing great. Now finish."

Stella leaned into Antonio's face as if she were going to kiss him but, instead, put her face right next to his ear and said, "Mr. Trovol, if you mess up your assignment in any way, I will find you and feed you to my fish. Look to your right. Piranha," she said sweetly, and then smiled.

Putting aside the shock he was feeling over Stella actually speaking to him, Antonio turned his head just enough to see a large fish tank and noted that it was oversized and plenty big enough to drop him in. Warner could see by the look on Antonio's face that his message was received loud and clear.

Antonio knew it was too late now, but this was not a man he wanted to work for or a job he wanted to take.

Pirates: Chapter 4

Crossing Boundaries

Peter was in his bedroom admiring the pictures that decorated the top of his dresser. There was one of his dad in a white frame with the words "Dad Loves You" across the top in big red letters. There was one from Disney World of Peter, his Mom, his little sister, Bell, and Tigger, who was the center of attention and giving them all a great big Tigger hug. But there was one photo that Peter couldn't take his eyes off of. Peter was just six years old when it was taken and he was sitting in a little red rocking chair with a huge smile on his face. In his arms he was holding his pet monkey, and on the top of the frame, scribbled in big blue letters, was "MONK".

Peter was starting to get really nervous and was pacing

around his room. He stopped for a second to peek out the window -- no one there. Then he walked across the floor to the door and looked out -- no one there. He shut the door and quickly opened it again -- no one there. Then he pretended like he was going to shut it and pulled it open really quickly -- still no one there.

"Where could he be?" Peter said with frustration. Peter was worried about Monk and the captain and he could only hope that they were both safe.

Captain Paul had chosen Peter as his first mate nearly two years ago. In this time, he and the captain had developed a strong bond, and this friendship meant a lot to Peter. Almost five weeks ago they had docked in the harbor and Peter had returned home to catch up on his school work and spend some time with his family. Now Peter was ready to get back out to sea and anxious to find out from Captain Paul where their next voyage would take them. But since returning home, Peter had not gotten a single communication from the captain, and Peter had begun to think that something might be wrong and the captain might be in peril.

When Peter had returned home, most of the crew had left on leave, with only Stanley the cook and Melvin, his helper, remaining on board. This made Peter very nervous. Despite extensive training, Stanley and Melvin were practically useless in battle and their skills with a sword were comical at best. However, they did show amazing promise in the kitchen, so that is where they were both assigned. But from time to time Stanley would still call Peter into the ship's galley and say,

"Look, Peter, watch this! I have been practicing my fighting skills."

Then Stanley would pull his sword from under the prep table, take his best fighting stance and pretend to do battle. By the time he finished his demonstration he had diced and spliced every vegetable he had laid out on the prep table. Stanley would then set down his sword in victory and ask, "What do you think, Peter?"

"Most impressive, Stanley," Peter would reply, smiling.

"I thought so," Stanley would say, all proud of himself.

"Keep up the good work, Stan."

Peter knew that doing battle with a head of broccoli and an army of Jersey tomatoes was very different than fighting a bunch of renegade pirates so, yes, Stanley and Melvin being the only two crew members left on the ship had Peter worried. But Peter was helpless to do anything from home and he couldn't go to the ship without being summoned -- that was Captain Paul's new rule. So what could he do? He thought about Monk. Peter had been sure that if he sent Monk to check on the captain that he would be doing the right thing, and yet no rules would be broken.

Monk's assignment was simply to get to the ship unseen and make sure the captain was safe. It seemed pretty basic to Peter and it certainly was nothing that Monk couldn't handle. Monk was a scout and could find a tick in the dark so this should be easy. According to Peter's time table, this task should have taken Monk no more than a few hours and, at the very longest, maybe a day. So by the second day of Monk being gone, Peter had started to worry and began talking to himself.

"This was such a simple assignment! Go look in on the captain and come home. How hard could this have been? Monk, where are you?"

By the sixth day, Monk was all that Peter could think about and he began to think the worst. The first thing that came to mind was something the captain had said to Peter the last time he saw him, and Peter's heart sank.

"The transporter!" Peter said out loud, his eyes growing wide with horror. The transporter could be faulty and, if it was, Monk could be anywhere.

Peter had known Monk for more than six years. He was not just one of the crew to Peter, he was his best friend in the world. Monk was a blue Indonesian Carma Monkey, a very rare breed found in the hills of Indonesia that had a limited ability to communicate with people. They were intelligent and had the brain function to learn and speak several hundred words, but Monk was smarter than most and his ability to learn was very impressive.

40

Monk had surpassed the language capabilities of most Carma Monkeys in the first year and now, on any given day, Peter had his hands full trying to get him to stop talking. From his blue color to his ability to speak, Monk was not your ordinary, run of the mill monkey, and this caught people's attention. Every now and then someone would get curious enough to ask Peter questions, the most common being, "What kind of animal is that?" Peter would always describe him the same way.

"He's a Carma Monkey from Indonesia and he is amazing! He's like a parrot with the abilities of a homing pigeon and the tracking skills of a bloodhound. This monkey could track down a deer tick in the middle of the forest, in the dark, while wearing Ray Ban sunglasses and listening to his iPod -- with his eyes shut." Peter would say this with great pride and it usually got a laugh in response, but all Peter was really doing was reciting the description that had been on the retail sales tag that came with Monk.

Peter loved Monk from the moment he spotted him. Ever since then, Monk has gone with Peter almost everywhere he goes, but there are some places, like school, that Monk just isn't allowed. When this is the case, Peter gives him a big hug, sets him on his bed, tells him to behave and that he will be back soon. Peter's mom has always reminded him to shut his bedroom door -- "Don't want Monk to get out," she would say.

But as much as Peter loved Monk and Monk loved Peter, they would sometimes battle like brothers, each one of them wanting things to turn out their own way. Monk could be frustrating at times and this usually got the best of Peter. He would lose his temper and start saying things that he shouldn't. Now that Peter is older, when he can't handle any more of Monk's antics he tries to remember what his mom has always told him -- "No one is without faults, Peter, so be patient. When you get frustrated, take a deep breath and exhale." Of course, this technique doesn't always work. But he does try.

Peter opened the bathroom door and turned on the light. He half expected to see Monk standing there, but he was not. Turning to face the bathroom mirror, Peter examined his new look. He had grown five inches in three months, making him, "Still shorter than me," his dad would say. Then he would laugh and rub Peter's head. Peter loved his dad, and every time he stood next to him he would smile and stand on his tippy toes to prove he was almost there. Peter calculated that if he grew five inches every three months that he would equal his dad's height within the next four months and surpass him in five.

Peter ran his fingers through his hair, brushing back the loose strands from his face. His body wasn't the only thing growing these days -- his hair had gotten so long that it hung down over his shoulders. His mom and dad

but the strange thing was that all the dreams ended the same -- with him reaching for a clear glass bottle that was corked shut. Inside the bottle was a note rolled up into a perfect cylindrical shape. The fact that the final image of every dream was exactly the same is what was bothering Peter. He was sure there was some meaning behind it.

The first dream had come to him on Monday night, the night that Monk had left for the ship. In the dream, Peter was floating in the sea on a raft made of bamboo. The shoots were tied together by shoelaces and the laces were all different colors. The sneakers that belonged to these laces were all tied to the four outer edges of the raft, like bumpers on a car. On top of the raft was a blue and yellow beach chair and a beach umbrella, sea blue with little yellow and red sun fish all over it, stuck out from the center of the raft. Peter was sitting on the edge of the raft kicking at the water when he spotted something bobbing along over the tops of the small waves. It was the clear glass bottle, corked shut, with the paper rolled up inside. Peter tried paddling with his hands to see if he could get close enough to grab the bottle. After a few minutes of hard paddling he made some headway and the bottle got closer and closer, until finally he was able to try to pull it out of the water. As Peter reached out to grab the bottle, his fingertips were almost touching it and then . . . Peter was sitting on his bed, wide-eyed in the dark, looking directly at his door. Peter had been disappointed when he realized he was still in his bedroom. He looked at the clock on his nightstand and it read 5:30 a.m. in big bright white numbers. Peter's stomach began to rumble and he was feeling a little hungry. This made him think of Stanley and how good his cooking was, and Peter just longed to be back on the ship.

Pirates: Chapter 5

Collecting Intelligence

Antonio sat in the very back of the pub at a small table by himself sipping a warm dark brew from a glass mug. On the table was a brown satchel and a stack of papers an inch thick. Antonio was reading and soaking up every single word that was written on these pages. The lighting in the pub was dim, which suited Antonio perfectly -- bright enough for him to work, yet dark enough so that anyone passing close to him couldn't see exactly what he was working on. For almost a week he had been reviewing all the information that Warner had given him, which included a diagram of the ship and a list of every man and woman on board with a brief description of what they looked like, where they came from and what their responsibilities were on the Rising Sea. In total there were fifty-two people on the ship when it was out at sea and, in Antonio's mind, that meant there were at least fifty-two ways this mission could go wrong. So before he risked his life for this job -- for a message in a bottle -- he would make sure he knew Delham's crew better than Delham himself.

At a glance the job appeared simple, like Warner had said, but no one could just walk onto a ship and stroll into a captain's quarters sight unseen; at least not without a plan. Antonio knew in his mind that no matter how easy something appeared, he could not let down his guard. He had to go to work prepared, and that meant knowing exactly what he was up against.

Warner's paperwork was thorough, with the only gap in information being the life history of a Peter Nichols, listed as the captain's first mate. The lack of information on this boy made Antonio uneasy and, adding to his feeling of concern, Peter was noted to be the owner of one of those strange little blue monkeys like the one that Warner had shown him. In Antonio's business it was important to be detail oriented and that meant making sure you crossed all your t's and dotted every i. Overlooking the smallest thing could create a dire situation and in the life history of Peter Nichols, there were no t's or i's to be found.

The other thing that was weighing on Antonio's mind was Warner's eagerness to get this job done. Antonio knew it would normally take more than fourteen days to come up with a solid plan of attack for a job such as this. Now he was going to be forced to rush the process to satisfy Warner's time requirement, leaving himself vulnerable. The ship had docked weeks ago and no new departure date was listed with the harbor master, so Antonio should have been able to take his time to plan the job correctly. But he had agreed to Warner's terms and now he would have to make sure that the job was completed on schedule -- his reputation was at stake.

The hardest part of this job now was trying to find a second man, someone he trusted but didn't know well. Warner all but said that whoever he chose needed to be disposable if the situation called for it and that didn't sit well with Antonio. It wasn't how he generally did business and he had no idea how he was supposed to pick someone trustworthy if he hardly knew the person. Antonio had stopped reading and was just staring at the pages trying to think this through when something caught his eye and startled him. Antonio looked up and, to his surprise, his nephew was standing in front of him.

"Marcus!" Antonio loudly exclaimed. "You scared me!" Antonio quickly flipped over the notes he was working on so they could not be seen.

"Uncle, you were so deep in thought that I wasn't sure it was you!" Marcus chuckled.

"What do you mean by that, lad?"

"My mother always tells my father that you are not much of a thinker, so I figured it couldn't be you sitting here so focused on something."

"Your mother says that, does she?"

"Every once in a while," Marcus said coyly.

"I bet it is more than once in a while."

"I bet you would be right."

"She was always a funny woman, your mother," Antonio said sarcastically. "She has never liked me, and I've never known why. I have always been very nice to her. Did she ever mention that I gave her solid gold candlestick holders as a wedding present?"

"Yeah, she tossed those in the trash years ago."

"What do you mean she tossed them in the trash?" Antonio said, sounding surprised.

"Well, when the gold started to rub off she said they were no better than cow dung and threw them out. At the time, I had heard her yelling something at my dad from across the house and I thought she was telling him how cheap and stingy he was. But now that I know you gave them the candlesticks, I guess she was talking about you."

Marcus couldn't hide his amusement and Antonio was starting to find his nephew as troublesome as his sister-in-law.

"Marcus, you are starting to bother me. What do you want, anyway?"

"I just came over to say hello, that's all."

"Well you said it and now we can say goodbye. I am working here and I need to get back to it."

"I didn't know you worked. What is it that you do?"

"Of course I work. Why would you think I didn't work?" Antonio curtly replied.

"My mother says that you're like a parasite and live off the kindness of others, so I assumed that work isn't your thing. I apologize. I must have misunderstood her."

Antonio quickly stood up from his chair, grabbed Marcus's shirt and leaned into his nephew. Marcus was caught off guard by his uncle's reaction and tried, unsuccessfully, to back away.

"I don't think you misunderstood her at all, lad," Antonio growled, "but I am starting to believe that when our Lord was handing out the common sense to know what is proper to say to another human being that you were left out of that line. Whatever your mother thinks of me is between her and me and is none of your concern, but what you should be worried about at the moment is how you're going to explain to your friends over there . . ." Antonio gave a wave to Marcus's drinking buddies across the pub, who were all watching him now, ". . .

53

why, in the middle of this fine establishment, I put my full grown nephew over my knee and gave him the spanking that his mother obviously never did. If I have personally offended you in some way then I suggest you tell me what I have done. If not, I suggest you stop living off your mother's bosom and be your own man. Do I make myself clear, lad?"

"Uncle Antonio, I was only kidding. Honestly. I just like to clown around a little," Marcus said a little shakily, trying to get free from his uncle's grasp.

"Well, Marcus, I am going to give you some worldly advice: find yourself a different source of amusement because that sort of clowning around is going to get you hurt." Antonio let go of Marcus and sat back down in his chair as Marcus took a step back, visibly shaken.

"I am truly sorry, Uncle Antonio. I don't know what else to say except let me buy you a drink and we can just start over."

"Marcus, I really . . ." Antonio started to reply.

"Don't say no, Uncle. I will be right back," interrupted Marcus.

Antonio could see Marcus talking to his friends at the bar and then the three boys left the pub. Marcus said something to the barkeep and then walked back over to Antonio with a pint in each hand. As Marcus got closer to his uncle he started to grin as if nothing had happened.

"Uncle Antonio, I've missed you," Marcus said. "Where have you been? It's been over a year since you've been in touch." Marcus gave Antonio a let's-be-friends kind of look.

Ignoring Marcus's question, Antonio replied, "Sit down, boy, you're making a fool of yourself."

"I do that every now and then."

"So I've noticed," Antonio said with a smile.

Marcus was twenty years old and the son of Antonio's eldest brother, the late Captain Dalti Trovol. Dalti had been very clumsy growing up so it didn't surprise Antonio at all when he had learned that his brother had fallen off of his horse and into the haunted ravine. Dalti had been missing for only a few weeks so there was a chance that he was still alive, but everyone was so afraid of the ravine that no one would go in to look for him and he was simply presumed to be dead. Antonio never really liked his brother -- Dalti was so opinionated about everything that it was hard to enjoy his company -- so even he didn't volunteer to look for him after the accident, despite being family. At the moment, Antonio just thought of Dalti as his late brother.

"Any recent news on your father, Marcus?" Antonio politely asked.

"Still missing. It has been almost four weeks now. Who would have ever thought that he would go like that?"

Antonio rolled his eyes and said, "Marcus, your father was the type of person who could have killed himself slow dancing in an empty room. It was a miracle that he survived as long as he did."

"He could still be alive, you know," Marcus retorted.

"Yes, he could," Antonio spoke out loud, while thinking that it *could* also snow in July.

Antonio preferred, for simplicity's sake, to consider his brother deceased until such time as Dalti walked himself out of the ravine. Although, after spending this time with Marcus, Antonio did have some doubts as to whether Dalti really was dead. Maybe his brother was just hiding from his crazy wife (finally realizing, after all these years, that she truly is); or maybe he recently spent a little time with his son and, discovering that crazy could be handed down to the next generation, was so overwhelmed that he leaped into the ravine intentionally just to get away from the two of them. This last thought made Antonio smile.

As they sat there together, Antonio found himself studying Marcus. Marcus's face looked like his mom's side of the family -- he had the Sicilian-Italian-meets-the-Greek-isles thing going on with the dark skin, piercing blue eyes and long dark hair. He also shared his mother's missing-all-the-aces-in-what-should-be-a-full-deck intelligence. In every other way, however, Marcus was his dad's son -- he was tall, thin and obnoxious, with

56

the unnerving ability to let every problem just run off of his back like nothing had ever happened. To Marcus, as to his father, the world was just one giant source of amusement. Take nothing seriously and there will be no consequences. But maybe Marcus's unrealistic view of the world was more a consequence of the example, or lack thereof, that his father had set. Suddenly Antonio couldn't help but feel that, as Marcus's uncle, it was now his responsibility to set Marcus straight, and what better way than to give him a job.

"Marcus, how would you like to work for me?" Antonio asked purposefully.

"You're joking, right?"

"No, actually, I am not. I have been looking for someone for a few weeks now and I have been unable to find the right man for the job." Antonio knew this was a lie, but it felt like weeks and he couldn't come up with anyone else.

"And you think that I am that man? Personally, I didn't think that we hit it off that well. Why would you want me to work for you?" asked Marcus.

"Earlier you said you wanted to know what I do for a living. Come work for me and I will show you what I do."

Marcus wasn't sure that he wanted to work for his uncle; he had other plans and they didn't include hanging out with Antonio. But the money wouldn't be a bad thing, and he was actually running a little low.

"What would I be doing for you?" Marcus asked cautiously.

"You would simply need to follow instructions and do exactly what I tell you to do. Can you do that?"

"It depends what it is. Like what?"

"I know this might sound vague, but I need someone to take care of problems that might come up while I am trying to work."

"What kind of problems?" Marcus persisted.

"People problems, for instance. I need someone who can handle people and possibly calm down a tense situation."

"I can do that," Marcus said, now getting more excited about the job offer. Dealing with people was something he thought he could do, and it didn't seem like very hard work, which made it even more appealing to Marcus.

"It is a big responsibility, lad, but I think you can handle it. Are you in?"

"Yes, I am," said Marcus. "When do I start?"

"Right now," said Antonio, as he gathered his belongings on the table and put them into his satchel. "Let's go."

Antonio threw the satchel over his shoulder and left the pub. Outside it was still light and there were people milling about, but the street was relatively quiet. Marcus trailed behind Antonio like a puppy dog, obediently following him without question. Neither of them spoke while Antonio led them out of the town. They were up the hillside on the outskirts of town before Marcus got curious.

"What are we doing out here, Unc?" he asked.

Antonio kept walking, but turned his head to reply. "Did you just call me 'Unc'?"

"Yes, it's short for uncle. It's easier to say."

"You need a shortcut for *Uncle*?"

"Yeah. Just in case I need to get your attention quickly, I can call you Unc," Marcus reasoned.

"Well I don't like 'Unc' and, as a matter of fact, don't call me Uncle, either. Just call me Antonio. People don't need to know that we're related."

"Okay, whatever," Marcus said as he rolled his eyes. "So, what are we doing out here, Ant?"

Antonio stopped walking, turned and stared at Marcus.

"What?" said Marcus. "It's short for Antonio."

"Lad, stop it with the abbreviations. My name is Antonio so just call me Antonio. Okay, *Mar*?"

Antonio turned away from Marcus and, looking ahead, he could now see the entire harbor from the hillside, including the Rising Sea alongside the dock. He put his telescope to his eye and surveyed the ship. From here he had a complete view of the entrance and deck.

"Fine, *Antonio*," Marcus answered. "What are we

doing up here?"

"Marcus, look into the telescope," said Antonio as he handed it to Marcus. "Do you see the dock?"

"Yes, the dock and all the pretty boats. There are seagulls too, Uncle Antonio," Marcus said with the wonderment of a little boy.

Antonio was trying his best to keep a cool head but Marcus was wearing down his patience. "Okay, follow the row of pretty boats all the way to the end of the dock until you can see the biggest one of all. Can you see it, Marcus?" Antonio said mockingly.

"Yes, I can see it. It's a nice ship. So what?"

"That is your job for the rest of the day -- watch that ship and keep track of how many people are on board. It has been docked for a while now so a lot of the crew are on leave, but I need to know who is on board at this time and what they look like."

"Why do you want to know what they look like?" asked Marcus.

"Don't worry about why. Just do it. And there is one particular boy that you need to keep an eye out for, his name is Peter Nichols and he is the captain's first mate."

"I have never met this boy, Antonio, so how in the world am I supposed to know who he is if I see him?"

"You will know him when you see him. He is the only crew member who will be in the company of a blue monkey," explained Antonio.

"Who owns a blue monkey?" Marcus said.

"First Mate Nichols, obviously, and if you see this monkey at any time you need to let me know immediately. Do you understand?"

"Aye, aye, sir," replied Marcus with forced earnestness.

"Listen, lad, I know you like to joke and I am giving you a little room to play here, but I have given you an important job and if you mess up it could create problems for us later, so please take it seriously."

Marcus looked at his uncle and in his most business-like manner said, "Antonio, if you want me to take this seriously then tell me what we are doing and why we are spying on that ship. What is the plan here? I think I have the right to know."

Antonio knew that his nephew was right. Marcus did need to know what to expect, but he would only tell him what was absolutely necessary.

"Marcus, I have been hired to deliver a package," Antonio offered.

"So why don't you just walk up to the boat like a normal person and hand it to the intended party?"

"It's a surprise package and the person who hired me wants to remain anonymous."

"Anonymous," repeated Marcus flatly.

"Yes, as in unknown. Marcus, most of the people who I work for do not like anyone to know their business and they all have their reasons. I work a lot and get paid very well because I don't ask questions. I don't know why the sender wants to remain anonymous. All I know is that this job requires you and me to take this package . . . ," Antonio paused as he removed the box with the bottle from his satchel and handed it to Marcus, "and set it on the desk of Captain Paul Delham. I know it sounds easy, but I have specific instructions that we must not be seen by anyone and that is why we need to know who is still on that ship."

Marcus looked thoughtfully at the box Antonio had handed him and asked, "What's in this box?"

"It is a simple gift from one man to another and that is all. You can look inside if you want."

Marcus flipped the lid open and saw in the box a clear bottle, corked shut, with a rolled up piece of paper inside it. "This is what you're getting paid to deliver?"

"Yes it is, lad."

Marcus could not believe that Antonio needed help delivering a simple bottle and, even more, that people where paying him to do it. The dollar signs started to flash in front of his eyes and, in an instant, any previous plans he had for his future were laid to rest with new ones now set in place. He decided he was going into the family business and, with that decision, Marcus picked up his own satchel and began to put the box inside.

"Marcus, what are you doing?" Antonio asked

suspiciously.

"I am putting the bottle in a safe place."

"My bag is perfectly safe," said Antonio as he reached for the box.

"Antonio, we are together on this right?"

"Yes, but . . . "

"No buts, Uncle. We are either together or we are not. If you don't trust me, then I should quit now."

Antonio hesitated before saying anything. He did need his nephew's help. He knew it and he was pretty sure that Marcus had sensed it. He realized that he had no choice, he had to trust him.

"It will be as safe in my bag as it was in yours, I promise. Trust me. After all, we're family," Marcus declared.

For Antonio, being family didn't do much to reassure him. "Okay, put it in your bag. Don't lose it."

Marcus slipped the box into his satchel and felt pretty good about himself at the moment. He had stood up to Uncle Antonio and he won.

Antonio continued, "Now you have to go to work, Marcus. Keep your eyes on that ship and write down a description of everyone you see. Write down whether the person was coming or going, if they were carrying anything. I need exact details. I will be back in a little while."

"Where are you going?"

"That is none of your business."

"But it will be dark soon. Then what?"

"By my calculations you have several hours of light left, Marcus. Let's see what you come up with in that time and I will let you know what we are doing next. I will be back at dusk."

With a hint of uneasiness in his voice, Marcus asked, "You are just going to leave me here by myself?"

"Yes, that is the plan."

"Well, what am I to use to take notes?"

Antonio hadn't thought of that. All he had was one quill and the pieces of parchment he had used to write his own notes on. As he thought about it more he was sure that there was nothing in his notes, or in his satchel for that matter, that would implicate Warner in any way. Since Marcus now had the bottle in his bag there was no need for Antonio to carry around his own satchel, so he set it down next to Marcus, who had made himself comfortable on the ground.

"Lad, I am putting a lot of faith in you here. In that satchel is everything you need. There is ink, a quill and some pieces of parchment. I have already written some notes of my own on them, but you can flip over the pages and write on the back sides. And lad, just one more thing."

"What is it?" asked Marcus, looking a little annoyed.

"Don't mess around with the package. It is safely in

your bag, so leave it alone. Got it?"

"Got it," said Marcus.

"Good," Antonio said with finality, then turned and walked away, leaving Marcus to attend to his job.

Antonio didn't really have anything else to do. He was used to working alone and he more or less was just a little tired of his nephew's company. Since it didn't take two people to watch one nearly empty ship, and sitting on that hard ground didn't seem like much fun, Antonio had decided that Marcus could do it. As he continued walking away, the rumble in his stomach reminded him that he hadn't eaten since breakfast. Suddenly the thought of a nice rare steak sounded really good, maybe with some mushrooms and sauted onions. He might even have some of those little red baby potatoes. Antonio picked up the pace and set his sights toward Magis Ale House for some dinner.

Pirates: Chapter 6

Sound of Silence

Stanley was a bald little man whose love of food helped him pack on the pounds -- two hundred and fifty of them, to be exact -- and, at five foot two, he was nearly as wide as he was tall. This extra weight took a lot of energy to move around, so after six weeks on the high seas, with fifty crew members to feed every day and Melvin to keep his eye on, he was burned out and just wanted to sleep.

Melvin was a bit wacky and, at times, a handful to control and Stanley couldn't help but wonder if he had been dropped on his head a time or two during his youth. But this boy came in very handy in the kitchen and there wasn't a shelf in the ship's pantry that he couldn't reach by just standing next to it. At six foot two, Melvin could reach up and touch the ceiling and, over time, Stanley figured that his head had made contact with every door jamb on the ship. And Melvin was as strong as he was tall -- Stanley hadn't lifted a sack, bucket or bushel in years thanks to Melvin. He was also amazing with steel wool. The pots and pans sparkled like they were encrusted with diamonds, not to mention you could eat off of the spotless floor. With all of this going for him, Stanley chose to overlook Melvin's bad qualities. Plus, Stanley just liked the lad.

As they pulled into port, most of the sailors foresaw weeks of excitement ahead. Stanley saw peace and quiet. Most of the crew couldn't wait to set foot into Harbor Ridge, but Stanley couldn't wait to sleep.

Harbor Ridge was a small costal town that wasn't located on any map and impossible to find unless you had the correct map coordinates. The crew liked to call it "Pirate Paradise," but it was simply the only town on an island inhabited mostly by pirates and their offspring. The town was filled with inns and taverns, the keepers of which had only one task -- to keep the sailors happy. One would think that an island inhabited by pirates would be a disorderly, disastrous place, but rules were set up by the town's board of overseers to discourage bad behavior and rule-breaking. Sailors docking here quickly discovered that the rules on this island were not made to be broken, and they were never broken twice. Captain Paul Delhem was one of the board members.

Once docked, Captain Paul slipped off the ship unnoticed, leaving his two attendees to look after things. Neither Stanley nor Melvin had their own families so they were more than happy to stay behind and watch the ship. The ship was their home and they both basked in the peaceful silence once every last man was gone.

After four weeks of being docked, Stanley and Melvin had grown very comfortable as the ship's keepers. The days passed without incident, but the thing Stanley had grown to love most were the nights -- the silent, calm and undisturbed nights. On one of these nights, Stanley was lying in his hammock, relaxed and listening to the sounds of the ocean. He loved hearing the wind whistle through the closed sails and masts and the waves slap against the sides of the ship. He closed his eyes and began to drift off to sleep.

"Stanley," whispered Melvin, "PSSSST, Stan. You awake? You awake?"

"No, Mel, I am sleeping, so leave me alone," Stanley quietly responded. *Silence and peace*, he thought to himself.

A minute went by without a sound.

"PSSSST, PSSSSSSST, Stan. Stanley," Melvin tried again. "You awake? I think I hear something."

"Melvin, if you stop talking there's a good chance the

only thing you'll hear is silence."

"No, I think I heard a creak."

"Are you kidding me? You woke me up because you think you heard a *creak*? We are on a ship, Mel. Everything on this ship creaks or bangs. If you listen close enough you can hear the pans in the galley."

"No, Stanley, it's not the ship. It sounded like footsteps."

"You can tell the difference between the creak of a board from a footstep and the creak of a mast, can you? I'm going back to sleep. Don't bother me again!" Stanley said angrily. *Silence and peace*, he said to himself again.

"There! There it is again!" urged Melvin. "Didn't you hear it?"

"That's it, Melvin. We are not going to do this again tonight! I didn't sign on to take care of a thirty year old man who's afraid of the dark. You have two choices at the moment: stop talking or go sleep in the galley. You choose."

"But, Stanley . . ."

Stanley did not wait to hear what Melvin was saying. "That is the last straw!" Stanley screamed. He rolled out of his hammock in a huff, waddled over to Melvin and grabbed the end of his hammock. With both hands, Stanley gave it one single hard tug, flipping Melvin onto the floor.

"Owwwww! That hurt! What did you do that for?" Melvin whined.

"Because you won't let me go to sleep!"

As Melvin got to his feet , Stanley grabbed him and began to drag him to the door.

"What are you doing, Stanley?"

"I am going to show you that this whole ship is creaking, that there is no one on board other than the two of us, and then, maybe, you'll let me go to sleep."

Stanley opened the cabin door and stepped out onto the deck with Melvin following right behind. Almost immediately, Stanley heard a clang, like the sound of a frying pan hitting the floor, and then a thump. Stanley turned quickly to see Melvin lying on the deck, then he heard a creak and . . . !

The sounds of a frying pan hitting something, a groan and a thump echoed into the night.

Pirates: Chapter 7

Still Dreaming

The first two dreams ending in the same manner didn't mean a lot to Peter. He had a lot on his mind and they were just dreams -- no big deal. By the fourth night, however, it was most definitely bizarre.

In the third dream, Peter had made his way up the beach to the harbor inlet. At the mouth of the inlet the beach stopped against a wall of large rocks. Leading from the wall was a path made of rocks that went out into the sea. These rocks were easy to stand on and a great place to sit and watch the boats come in. Peter had found the perfect rock to fish from; one large enough for his tackle box and a beach chair and, if he hooked anything worth bragging about, it was big enough that he wouldn't get pulled into the water.

The sun was hot and Peter was sitting in the beach chair with his line cast into the ocean. He had the fishing pole balancing between his two knees when he felt the line tighten and saw the pole bend. A sign that he had hooked something, Peter took the pole with both hands and gave the line a slight tug but the pole bent even further. Peter worked hard to bring in his catch. He reeled and pulled and reeled some more and the harder he reeled and pulled, the harder the struggle became. Finally, with one last tug, Peter's catch came flying out of the water and was dangling just inches from the edge of the big rock he was standing on. But at the end of the line was not a big tuna or swordfish flailing to get away. Instead there was a bottle -- a clear glass bottle that was corked shut with a piece of paper rolled up inside. Peter set down the fishing pole and pulled at the line, hand over hand, to bring the bottle closer. The bottle made a clinking sound as it gently bounced across the rock which stopped when it came to rest at Peter's feet. Peter reached down to pick up the bottle and as his hand wrapped around the bottle's neck . . ..

Peter's eyes opened and he was again sitting up in bed, looking directly at the back of his bedroom door. Yet again, for the third time in as many nights, he felt a twinge of disappointment. It was only 4:02 a.m. but again his stomach rumbled and he wished he could raid the galley refrigerator and chow down some left over chicken cutlets with Stanley's homemade potato fries.

Pirates: Chapter 8

Details Part I

Stanley opened his eyes. He was dizzy and dis-oriented, and he had the worst headache he had ever experienced. He went to reach for his head and discovered that his arms were tied against his torso and he was lying on his side on the cold floor. The sound of someone moaning was coming from behind him. Suddenly it all came rushing back and he remembered the creak and the bang, every last detail, then -- Melvin!

"Melvin, can you hear me? Mel, are you okay?" Stanley said in a shaky voice.

But Melvin did not answer. He was still out cold.

Stanley lifted his head to look around and could just

make out that they were in the food pantry. He tried to move his body to get a better look and that is when he realized that he and Melvin were tied together, back to back. His feet were tied together, so he couldn't move his legs, and his hands were tied, as well. Stanley struggled to free himself but the ropes were too well knotted.

"Pssst, Melvin, can you hear me?" Stanley tried again.

Melvin just moaned.

Stanley was helpless and he knew it. He let his head drop to the floor and closed his eyes. Almost immediately, he heard a creaking sound coming from the galley. Stanley's eyes grew as wide as a hoot owl's and then he noticed that he could see under the pantry door and into the galley. The creaking was getting louder and closer. Stanley's heart started pounding and he heard that the sound was coming towards the pantry door. Then it stopped and, from Stanley's vantage point, he could see two boots.

"Footsteps," acknowledged Stanley to no one but himself. Stanley was feeling angry with himself. He couldn't believe Melvin had been right about the footsteps and, for some reason, he felt the need to tell him.

"Melvin!" Stanley screamed, hoping his friend would hear him. "Footsteps, Melvin. Footsteps!"

The door burst open and, over the sound of the wind

75

and the ocean, there was a sharp ring as a sauce pan hit Stanley's skull. The last thing he saw before he blacked out were two boots, each one with a single silver skull on it.

"Lights out," Marcus said laughing as he looked down at Stanley on the floor.

Pirates: Chapter 9

Lights Out and Sweet Dreams

On the seventh night of Monk's absence, Peter leaned over to turn off the lights and looked out the window. He could see the night sky filled with twinkling stars and a full moon. He slid into bed sideways, the bed squeaking under his weight, and fell backwards until his head hit his pillow with a thud. He pulled the covers up to his chest and looked up at the ceiling. He was thinking about Monk, and started worrying about how he would feel if something happened to him -- it would be Peter's fault and it wouldn't feel good.

Peter had been second guessing himself for days. Maybe sending Monk to the ship had been a bad idea, he thought. But he couldn't go himself, that was for sure. He would have gotten into serious trouble with Captain Paul if he were caught. But Peter had not heard from Paul in five weeks and he found that odd. Was he wrong to want to make sure the captain was safe? He didn't think so at the time. Peter's only concern when he decided to send Monk to the ship was making sure that he didn't break rule number 1702 of the Pirate's Log more than he already had.

Yes, he *had* broken it, even in not going to the ship himself, and Peter knew the captain would be angry with him, but he just hadn't been able to bring himself to destroy the boots. Oh, he did try. He even made Monk wristbands from the leather he cut off the top two inches of each boot while he was trying to destroy them. That was how Monk was able to transport to the ship by himself. Peter didn't know it at the time, but the boots didn't need to be intact to work -- any part of the boot became a transport. Peter had watched in shock the day Monk put on his new wristbands and disappeared. The captain must have known this, too, because he had wanted Peter to destroy the boots while he was still aboard the ship the last time he was there.

Captain Paul had given Peter a brand new pair of boots the day he was leaving for home. He told Peter they were to replace the old ones and then told him to pitch the old boots into the fire but, at that exact moment, Nic called out from the crow's nest and the captain got distracted. When he turned his back on Peter to talk to Nic, Peter swapped a spare pair of old black gym sneakers from his knapsack for the boots and quickly tossed the sneakers into the flames. By the time the captain turned back around the shoes were pretty well burned up and Peter's boots were safe. The captain had looked at Peter, put his hand on his shoulder and said,

"I'm sorry, lad, but it had to be done."

And Peter had bowed his head -- in shame.

When Peter had decided to send Monk to check on Captain Paul, all Peter kept thinking was that Monk wasn't factored into the captain's new rule so no harm, no foul, right? It had never dawned on Peter that Monk might end up in danger too, but now Monk was gone and Peter couldn't stop worrying. So, as Peter lay there, safe in his own bed, he wasn't finding any comfort in the fact that he had skirted the captain's rule. He hadn't stopped to think of Monk's safety and he was feeling like a really bad friend.

After a long hard battle within himself, Peter decided that he had to man up and tell Captain Paul about the boots. Captain Paul will certainly be angry but, worse than that, what weighed down Peter's heart the most was knowing that he might lose the captain's trust. Peter's stomach turned sour. He took a deep breath and rolled onto his side to stare out the window.

It had been nearly an hour since Peter had climbed into bed and this heavy emotional battle finally wore him out. His eyes got heavy and he began to drift off. The last conscious thought Peter had was that at first light he was going back to the ship -- Rule 1702 be darned! -- to find his friend Monk and bring him home.

Pirates: Chapter 10

Details Part II

Marcus walked out of the pantry holding a sauce pan with a smile on his face.

"Marcus, what happened in there?" Antonio asked.

"I was taking care of one of those people problems."

"We shouldn't be having any people problems," Antonio said, scowling.

"The chubby fellow woke up and started screaming." Marcus held up the pan for Antonio to see, and continued, "This quieted him right down." Marcus stifled a chuckle.

"Did he see you?" Antonio asked with a hint of alarm

in his voice.

"It's dark enough in there that I wouldn't recognize my own mama," Marcus replied.

"I don't care who recognizes your mama, Marcus. Did he see you?" Antonio demanded.

"No, he didn't, okay?"

"No, it's not okay. I thought I told you to blindfold and gag them?" Antonio asked, clearly agitated.

"You did, but I forgot. Shoot me," Marcus said sarcastically.

"If only I could," Antonio murmured to himself.

Then, grabbing Marcus by the shirt collar, Antonio pulled him close enough to whisper in his ear, "Listen to me, and listen closely. We are here to do a job. Part of that job is making sure that no one sees us or discovers we were here, at least not until after we are far from this ship. So when I tell you to blindfold and gag a man, you need to do exactly that. You cannot forget. It is missing little things like that, those seemingly tiny little details, that will get us killed. Do you understand, Marcus?"

"Yes, I got it. It won't happen again."

"Good to hear," said Antonio, "now give me the bottle. Let's finish this job and get out of here."

Marcus reached into his satchel and began to fish around for the bottle.

"Boy, give me the *bottle*," Antonio repeated.

Marcus hesitated a second before replying, "It's not

there."

"What do you mean it's not there?"

"I searched twice and only the box is in the bag. The bottle is gone."

Trying to remain calm, Antonio said, "It couldn't have just disappeared. When was the last time that bag was off of your shoulder?"

Marcus thought a moment before replying, "The deck. I set it down to pop the cook and his friend." Marcus frowned as he remembered, and continued, "I kicked it! I accidently kicked the bag. The bottle must have rolled out."

It was dark and hard to see the look on Antonio's face, but Marcus knew exactly what he was about to say. Even before the words came out of his uncle's mouth, Marcus said, "I know, Antonio, it's one of those tiny little details."

"No, Marcus," Antonio seethed, "that is *not* a tiny little detail. That is a catastrophically *huge* detail. That bottle is why we are here!"

Antonio felt as though he might explode, but he knew that losing his temper would not solve their problem. He turned away from Marcus, opened the galley door and stepped onto the deck, looking into the night -- even the moon and stars were not bright enough tonight to assist in their search.

Pirates: Chapter 11

Monkey Troubles

Antonio knew that walking around the deck with a torch or a lantern in the middle of the night might draw unwanted attention, and searching for the bottle in the dark was hopeless. They would have to bunk down for the night.

Antonio pushed his way past Marcus and said, "You get first watch. I'm going to catch some sleep." Antonio lay down on the galley floor.

"When should I wake you?"

"When the sun comes up, that's when."

Marcus, sounding annoyed, said, "When do I sleep, when is your watch?"

"You lost the bottle, my boy, so you get the first and only watch tonight."

Marcus didn't like this at all but he knew it was not an argument that he was going to win so he left it at that. Morning could not get here soon enough, he thought.

As the sun was coming up over the horizon it was deep orange in color, indicating that the day would be a hot one. The aroma of Stanley's beef stew still filled the galley from the night before and his homemade apple pie sat on the cutting table inviting someone to slice into it. Antonio was still fast asleep, snoring away, and Marcus, while still on watch, was sound asleep as well. That was until he was startled by a noise on the deck; then he was awake in an instant. He wiped the sleep from his eyes and tried to get his bearings -- it took him a few seconds to remember where he was. As he looked around the galley, he could tell by how light it was that he had been sleeping for some time.

"This is bad," Marcus said to himself.

He knew Antonio was not going to be happy. It had to be mid-morning by now; they should have found that bottle hours ago and been long gone already. Then he heard the noise again and realized that someone else was on the ship. Marcus opened the galley door just wide enough to take a peek of the deck, and it took only a second to see all that he needed to. He had to wake Antonio.

85

With his hand over Antonio's mouth, Marcus said softly, "Antonio, wake up. Wake up!"

Antonio's eyes opened and grew wide. His first reaction to the hand over his mouth was to fight for his life, but he instantly saw that it was Marcus and calmed down.

In a whisper, Marcus said, "Antonio, someone is on the ship."

"Who is it?" said Antonio.

"It's the boy's monkey."

"What boy? The captain's first mate?"

"Yes," said Marcus, "it's the blue monkey you told me about."

"Is the boy with him?"

"No, it's just the monkey. What should we do?"

"Marcus, what was the monkey doing when you saw him?" Antonio could read the panic on Marcus's face. "Marcus," Antonio repeated, "what was he doing?"

Marcus took a deep breath. "He was looking at the bottle."

"*What*?" Antonio said in a horrified whisper.

"The bottle," Marcus said again.

"Our bottle? The one you had insisted was safely stashed in your bag before you lost it?" Antonio growled.

"Yes, that one."

Antonio rushed to the door and silently opened it,

careful not to draw attention to themselves.

"Is he still there?" Marcus asked.

Antonio just glared at him.

It was indeed the monkey. A blue Carma Monkey just like the one on Warner's ship, and Antonio remembered clearly what had taken place on the ship. He also remembered what Warner had said to him about Peter Nichols's monkey -- "He is not a normal monkey, Antonio. He can communicate just like you and I so don't let him see you." Antonio closed the door and stepped away from it.

"What are we doing?" asked Marcus.

"Nothing. We are doing nothing."

"What do you mean we're doing nothing? We can't just sit here. We need to get that bottle back."

"Yes, we can just sit here, Marcus. We can't leave this galley until that monkey leaves the ship."

"That doesn't make any sense! It's just a monkey."

"No, it's not *just* a monkey. It's a Carma Monkey."

"I don't care if it's a chimpanzee in a grass skirt. Let's go get the bottle and get this done," said Marcus impatiently.

"We can't. The monkey can talk."

Marcus looked at Antonio like he was insane. "Have you been nipping at the cooking sherry, Antonio? I looked all over this kitchen last night to see if that cook had a bottle and I couldn't find any. I should have known that you found it and kept it for yourself, but you didn't have to drink the whole bottle at once."

"There is no sherry and I haven't been drinking anything, Marcus. I'm telling you the truth. I know it sounds crazy, but Warner showed me one and, sure enough, it talked."

"Warner? Who is Warner?"

Antonio had felt the name slipping off of his tongue and yet he could not stop himself in time. Now Marcus had heard the name and Antonio could only hope that he didn't put a face to it.

"He's a friend of mine. No one you would know, but he has one of these monkeys and showed it to me."

Marcus sat down on the floor, trying to wrap his head around the idea of a talking monkey. "I have never heard of such a thing," said Marcus skeptically. "Where are they from?"

"I think he said Indonesia."

"You're pulling my leg, right?"

Taking a deep breath, Antonio said, "Marcus, ask yourself why I would choose to stay locked up in this galley with you if I could just walk out there right now and get the bottle back. Of course I'm being serious. Now, this is what I am thinking -- you have been up all night and are probably tired. When people get tired they start to make mistakes, and I don't need for you to make any more mistakes than you already have."

Marcus cringed at this comment.

Antonio continued, "You should get a wink or two now and I will take watch. I will wake you if the situation changes. Okay?"

"Okay, if that's what you want me do. Thanks," Marcus replied, trying to sound sincere.

Of course, Marcus was not tired in the least, but he decided that pretending to sleep was probably his best bet at this point. He almost had to be thankful for the monkey's timing -- if it stayed long enough it was possible that Antonio would never figure out that he had fallen asleep when he was supposed to be on watch. Marcus wanted Antonio to teach him his business and he was sure a mistake of this gravity would put an end to that dream. He could only hope that no one else showed up and made the situation worse.

While Marcus feigned sleep, he heard Antonio grumbling under his breath occasionally, and when he peeked through slitted eyes, he could see Antonio opening and shutting the galley door to check on the monkey. After a couple of hours of this, the hard floor started to hurt and Marcus had enough of pretend sleeping. He sat up and looked around. There was an aroma wafting through the galley that caught his attention and Marcus was trying to figure out what he was smelling. Whatever it was, it was making him hungry.

Pirates: Chapter 12

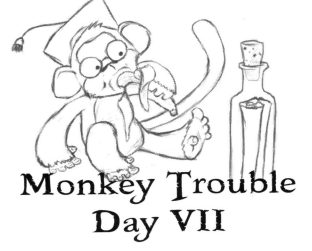

Monkey Trouble Day VII

Day one came and went, as well as days two, three, four, five and six. By day seven Antonio was ready to throw in the towel. Six days of hiding in the galley with two prisoners presented many problems, some with solutions that even a pirate would find disgusting.

Antonio was peering out the door on the morning of the seventh day, checking to see if Monk was still there, when Marcus asked,

"What's he doing now?"

"Same thing he's been doing for the last six days -- eating bananas and staring at our bottle," an exasperated Antonio replied.

"Is he in the same place or has he moved?"

"He hasn't moved since Monday," Antonio marveled. "He's like a statue that eats."

Monk had only changed his location on the ship once in seven days and that was to go from the deck into the crow's nest on the day he had first arrived. Monk had stayed in the crow's nest because he had a better view of the whole ship from up there, but he could also keep an eye on the bottle lying on the deck below him. To Antonio and Marcus, Monk just seemed to be fascinated with the bottle but, in reality, he was keeping watch for the captain. Finding the bottle on the deck seemed a bit strange to Monk, and there had been no sign of Stanley or Melvin since he got there, which was even stranger. Monk had a feeling something was wrong, and he thought the bottle had something to do with his uneasy feeling, so he hadn't taken his eyes off of the bottle all week.

"We are going to die here you know," Marcus said flatly.

"*You* can die here, Marcus. I have other plans."

"Yeah, and what kind of plans do you have?"

"Well, if you *don't* die here, feeding you to the alligators is the first thing on my list, boy, and I don't care what your mother has to say about it. I am going to do it nice and slow, too. I'll dangle you above them so they can jump up and eat you a little bit at a time."

"Nice, that is really nice, Antonio."

"Marcus, that monkey has been eating bananas for six straight days. Where is he getting them from?" Antonio wondered, clearly frustrated.

"A tree," replied Marcus sarcastically.

Antonio rolled his eyes and continued, "He hasn't left that nest once."

"He must have them stashed up there," Marcus reasoned.

"There can't be enough room in that lookout to hold the amount of bananas he has eaten in the last six days," Antonio persisted.

"If I ate that many bananas I would be filled with so much gas that you wouldn't want to be in the same room as me," said Marcus, clearly amused with himself.

"I don't want to be in the same room as you now," remarked Antonio. "Look! He's eating another banana. *Where* is he getting them?"

Antonio just could not stop talking about the bananas and it was starting to get to Marcus. He was bored and couldn't stand being in the galley anymore. In six full days they had consumed almost everything that was edible and the nice beef smell that had been here when they arrived had been replaced by the odor of rotting garbage. Not to mention the natural scent of four grown men who had been cooped up in a hot room together and hadn't bathed in a week. It was downright nasty.

"He's moving, he's coming down from the crow's

nest!" Antonio excitedly announced. "Hmm, I never noticed that before but he has a satchel. What does a monkey need a satchel for?"

"To carry his bananas?" Marcus mockingly asked.

"Ha, ha, ha," said Antonio, clearly not amused. "I think he's leaving. He's heading to the gangplank."

Antonio continued looking through the cracked open galley door and, after a minute or two had passed, Marcus wanted to know what was happening.

"Is he gone?"

"No, not yet," Antonio offered. "He's standing on the gangplank looking out towards the dock."

Then Antonio watched in horror as Monk ran back to their bottle, quickly stuffed it into his satchel and ran down the gangplank. He wanted to scream, "Nooooooo, don't!" but it wouldn't come out. Instead, Antonio just stood there with a pained expression that looked like he had just been shot.

"Antonio, are you okay? What's wrong?" Marcus wanted to know.

Antonio opened up the galley door and stepped out on the deck, staring at the spot were the bottle used to be. Marcus followed Antonio out and stood by his side. As he followed his stare, Marcus's eyes bulged and he became instantly sick.

Pirates: Chapter 13

Taken to the Edge

The dreams kept coming and on night seven Peter found himself building castles in the sand. He had built three cities of castles and each city was surrounded by moats and drawbridges. The castles were enormous -- the bigger the better, he thought. Peter had his old Star Wars action figures guarding the castles, with Sleeping Beauty in the tower and the prince, on his horse, fighting the ogre and the evil donkey. There were eight sand buckets lined up on the beach, each one a different size and each more colorful than the next. He had just finished laying down his final drawbridge and filling up the moats with water when the ocean rushed up the beach and covered his feet. Peter looked down and saw a bottle right next to his foot. He reached down to pick it up and noticed a piece of paper rolled up inside the bottle. As Peter started to wrap his fingers around the bottle . . . Peter opened his eyes and was startled by a dark figure sitting directly in front of him.

Peter screamed, "Ahhhhhhhhhhhh!"

The figure in front of Peter also started to scream. "Ahhhhhhhhhhhhh!"

Then Peter screamed, "Ahhhhhhhhhhhh!" again.

Then the shadow. "Ahhhhhhhhhhhh!"

Then they both stopped screaming at the exact same moment and just stared at each other. Peter's eyes began to adjust to the darkness and the shadow became clearer.

"Monk, is that you?"

"It is."

"Monk," said Peter cautiously, "is this a dream?"

"I don't think so," said Monk. "How can you tell?"

"I think I know how," said Peter, as he reached his hand out. In every other dream Peter had had this week, he would wake up every time he reached out to touch the bottle with the paper inside. So Peter reached for the bottle and when his fingertips touched the glass . . . he didn't wake up. He was already awake and the bottle felt hard and quite real.

"Monk, I can feel the bottle! I can actually touch it!" Peter exclaimed.

"I can see that Peter. Haven't you ever touched a bottle before?" Monk asked, unimpressed.

"Yes, I have touched bottles before. It's not about touching the bottle," Peter answered impatiently.

"Peter, you've lost me. Can you get to the point?"

"Monk, I have been having dreams all week while you've been gone and, at the end of each dream, I would try to pick up a bottle just like the one you're holding. Just as I was about to touch it, I'd wake up, and tonight when I woke up you were sitting there with the bottle, so I wasn't sure if either you or the bottle was real. You see, the first night I was floating on a raft, and then. . ."

"Peter, Peter, please stop, okay?" interrupted Monk. "I get it. You had some dreams about a bottle, and I don't mean to sound rude or uninterested, but I really hate hearing about people's dreams. There is usually no structure or direction of any sort in a dream -- they are all over the place, they never make any sense and, in my opinion, they are badly directed by the dreamer. Would you pay money to go see a movie that was so badly directed that it didn't make sense? No, I don't think you would. So why do people think anyone wants to hear about their badly directed dreams, even for free?"

Peter gave Monk a nasty look. He hated when his friend did this type of thing. Monk was being dismissive and it bothered him. How many times did Peter have to listen to Monk's adventures, and did Monk really think that his stories of how he found the best banana trees were of any interest to him? "I don't think so," thought Peter, "but at least I have the decency to pretend I'm listening!" Peter wanted to say this out loud to Monk but, instead, wanting to avoid an argument, simply said,

"Okay, Monk, I get that you don't want to hear about my dreams. So just tell me, then, where you got that bottle from?"

"You told me to go to the ship and spy on the captain so you would know what he was doing. That is exactly what I did and when . . ."

"Wait a second! I didn't tell you *spy* on him! I told you to see if he was there and come back and let me know."

"No, Peter, you are wrong. I'm sure you used the word 'spy'," Monk said indignantly.

"No, never! I never told you to spy on him. I was worried about him because I hadn't heard from him in weeks and I asked you to just look in on him," Peter insisted.

"So, Peter, what you're saying to me is you didn't use the word 'spy'?"

"No, Monk, I did not!"

"Are you sure, Peter, because it definitely felt like spying to me."

"Monk, I don't care what it felt like. I assure you that I did not send you there to spy on anyone."

Monk thought about what Peter was saying for a few seconds and then looked around the dark room as if someone else might be listening. Then Monk's face lit up like a lightbulb and, with his eyes opened wide, he leaned into Peter and whispered softly into his ear, "Oh, I get it. I get it."

Monk then backed away and started talking in his loudest speaking voice, overemphasizing each word like a bad actor in a stage play, "Oh, I remember now, Peter. Right, right, you *didn't* say spy." Then Monk winked at Peter and smiled.

Peter jumped out of bed, knocking Monk backwards, and turned on the lights. When Peter turned back around to look at Monk he was glaring and, in the most sarcastic tone he could muster up, Peter said, "Where in the world did I get you from!"

"Well," said Monk, sounding slightly offended. "Where did you get me from? I have to say, Peter, it has been a long time and I'm not sure I really remember. I know it wasn't Jumbo-Mart because the company that made me couldn't meet their quantity requirements -- five hundred thousand pieces, Peter! Can you believe that? -- and Jumbo-Mart wanted the right to return any unsold items. Those conditions are just crazy! Who can do business like that? But, anyway, don't you have my receipt?"

"What? No, I don't!" Peter yelled.

"Well, you should really get into the habit of keeping receipts, you know. You never know when you might need them."

"Like if I need to return defective merchandise?" Peter said pointedly.

"Exact . . . ly," Monk stammered. He looked thoughtful, a little bit hurt, even, but after a few seconds he broke out into a belly laugh as though Peter had just told him the funniest joke ever. "Peter, you almost had me there with the returning of the merchandise thing! I was worried for a second. You are a funny guy!"

Peter took a deep breath. "Monk, stop please. Seriously, now, I need to know where you got that bottle with the note in it."

Monk looked thoughtful again. He squinted his eyes as he went into a deep train of thought that seemed to last forever, and then hollered out, "Target!"

Peter looked confused and said, "You got the bottle at Target? The department store Target?"

"No, not the bottle. Me, Peter. I think you got *me* at Target. I distinctly remember that there was a fundraiser going on for some needy children or something and I was sitting right across from the fundraiser stuffed animals when you came strolling up the aisle with your mom. You were touching everything in the store -- I thought your mom was going to kill you -- and then you walked up to me and you picked me. I couldn't believe

99

it! Out of all the animals in the world, you picked *me*!"
Monk gave Peter a big toothy smile and Peter took
another deep breath.

"Monk, at this moment I am finding it very hard to
believe that I picked you myself."

"I know," said Monk, ignoring Peter's meaning, "it
was like it was meant to be."

Suddenly the expression on Peter's face changed and
his voice had a sense of urgency. "Monk, I got it! I think
I know!"

"Know what?" asked Monk.

Peter didn't answer. He just quickly walked over to
his closet, reached up to the top shelf and pulled down a
blue shoe box with two thick rubber bands wrapped
around it to keep the lid from falling off. He pulled off
the rubber bands, flipped the top off of the box and began
rifling through the contents.

"Peter, what are you looking for? Can I help? What
is all this stuff?" Monk asked.

"I've got it!" announced Peter. "I've got it! I can't
believe it, but it came to me -- it just popped into my
head -- and I knew. I knew just where to look."

"What is it, Peter, what did you find?"

"Bon Ton!" yelled Peter.

Monk looked scared, but then, excitedly, continued
with his questions, "Bonton? What's Bonton, Peter? Is
it a secret password? Is it a clue? Does it tell you where

to find Captain Paul? Peter, please tell me, what does it mean? What is Bonton?"

Peter looked at Monk and laughed. "Monk, it is not a secret code or a password, but I am hoping that it will help me find the captain."

"Peter, what is it?"

"It is a department store, Monk!"

"It sounds familiar," said Monk, but he wasn't sure why and now he was confused. "A department store? Why were you looking for a department store?"

"I wasn't looking for the store," Peter said. "I was looking for this."

Peter held up a small white piece of paper with a bunch of words and numbers on it. At the top, typed in large black but somewhat faded letters, it read:

The Bon • Ton

Phillipsburg, NJ

"It's your receipt, Monk. I did keep the receipt. Look! You cost $31.99 but we got you on sale for $15.99, along with a package of Fruit of the Loom tighty whities and a Yankees baseball cap, and look, at the bottom of the receipt. Do you see that?"

Peter held the receipt in front of Monk so he could read it and pointed at the words on the bottom.

"Just in case you missed any of it, let me read it to you: 'All merchandise may be returned if accompanied by the receipt'. Now, Monk, I grew out of the underwear some time ago, so they are long gone, and the Yankees hat has a huge white sweat stain around the brim, so I don't think they will take that back, but you know what? You're still in pretty good shape, Monk, so if you don't tell me where you got that bottle from *right now* I am going to be fifteen dollars and ninety-nine cents richer. Do you understand what I am saying here? Now, where did you get that bottle?" Peter demanded.

Monk had to admit that he had never seen Peter this angry and hostile in all of the years they had been together. He found himself at a loss for words, which almost never happened. Monk read the dictionary daily and yet he couldn't think of any words for the perfect retort. All he could come up with was, "Wow!"

It took Monk a minute to regain his train of thought before he spoke again. "Peter, you didn't have to resort to blackmail. I was going to tell you anyway. What has happened to you? Friends don't use blackmail as a means to get what they want. What is that about?"

"I want the bottle, Monk, and I want to know where you got it," Peter replied simply.

"I can't believe our relationship has gone so wrong," Monk said without looking at Peter. "I am really hurt, you know, and I may have to rethink our friendship. I think there is a chance that it is just not working out anymore."

Monk looked at Peter with the saddest eyes and Peter

could see how much he had actually hurt his friend's feelings.

"Okay, Monk, I'm sorry," said Peter. "I am really sorry. What I did was probably unforgivable, and I feel bad about it. But the bottle was in my dreams and now you have it -- it's real! -- and I just wanted to know where you got it from, but you just . . ."

"It's okay, Peter." Monk was holding up his hand, indicating for Peter to stop talking. "I forgive you. I know you're stressed, you just woke up, your sugar levels are probably out of balance and those fragmented dreams can get to . . ."

It was Peter's turn to interrupt. "Monk, please focus -- the bottle!"

"It's amazing, Peter. When you get locked into one topic you just can't let it go, can you?"

Monk could see Peter was getting annoyed again and smiled at him. Then he answered, "The ship. I found the bottle on the ship. I walked up the gangplank and there it was, sitting on the deck. You would have to have been blind to miss it, and if you were you would have tripped over it."

"Well, why didn't Captain Paul pick it up then?" said Peter.

"The captain wasn't on the ship. As a matter of fact, nobody was on board. It was empty," explained Monk.

Peter's look of concern was most obvious. "Empty?"

"Yes, empty," repeated Monk, "as in vacated, unoccupied, uninhabited . . ."

"Monk, I know what empty means," Peter tried to interject.

". . . abandoned, deserted and, most definitely, vacant."

"Stop!" said Peter. "If you don't stop doing that I am going to take the dictionary away from you."

Monk started to laugh. He reached into his knapsack, pulled out the dictionary and proudly said, "I have been working on my synonyms. I thought you would be impressed."

"Well, yes, it is most impressive, Monk," said Peter, "but it is also very annoying, and if you look up the word annoying you will see that it is not a good thing or an endearing attribute."

Peter took a very deep breath and exhaled. Monk used the sudden pause in conversation to get acquainted with this new word, quickly thumbing his way through his dictionary until he found what he was looking for.

"Annoying," Monk said excitedly, pointing to the word, and then read the definition silently, in his head: to disturb or bother a person in a way that displeases, troubles, or irritates. The excitement in Monk's face was replaced with a frown.

"I don't like this word," said Monk.

"I told you it wasn't a good thing," said Peter.

Monk, looking a bit put out, said, "Yes, yes you did, and your point has been made. Now, can we move on?"

"Yes," said Peter, "that's a good idea."

Monk then made a mental note to look up the words "endearing" and "attribute". Peter had used them in the same sentence with "annoying" so he wasn't sure that he was going to like those words either.

"So, Monk, if no one was on the ship, why did you stay there for a whole week? What were you doing? You had me worried sick!" Peter continued where they had left off.

Monk responded, a bit defensively, "You said you wanted to know what the captain was doing. That was the assignment you gave me, so I figured you would want me to stay as long as it took to finish the job. I stayed on the ship keeping watch for the captain, but this morning, while I was in the crow's nest having breakfast -- you know, I found the greatest banana tree . . ."

Peter, remembering their earlier dream conversation, wanted to tell Monk that he never wanted to hear another story about bananas again, but Peter bit his lip so that Monk could continue.

". . . and when I looked down and that bottle was still sitting in the middle of the deck, it really started to bother me, so I thought the best thing to do was to bring it back to you and see what you thought. If you want me to take it back to where I found it, I will."

Then Monk, holding the bottle, started to walk toward the door.

"Stop, stop, stop! Monk, you know very well I don't want you to take it back. What I want to do right now is crack open that bottle and see what that note says. What do you say, Monk? Can I open that bottle and read the note?"

Monk thought about it for a second and started to hand Peter the bottle but, just as Peter reached for it, he stopped and pulled it back.

"Don't play with me, Monk!" Peter protested.

"I am not playing with you, Peter, but if I give you this bottle, I want something in return."

Peter looked shocked. "What do you mean you want something in return?"

"I mean I want something in return, as in I give you the bottle and you give me whatever I ask you for."

"Monk, that is just silly. It is not your bottle to be bargaining with, and that note inside could be a clue to finding Captain Paul. You are wasting valuable time."

Calmly, Monk replied, "Peter, this bottle is more mine than it is yours because I found it and, for all we know, Captain Paul does not want to be found. All I want, in exchange for the bottle, is to ask you something and I want you to give me an honest answer."

Peter felt like Monk was pushing him toward the edge of a cliff and he just wouldn't stop. Peter was taking so many deep breaths in an effort to keep his cool that it was making him dizzy. It was only a matter of time before his anger would get the best of him but, for now, Peter managed to respond to Monk with only the slightest edge to his voice,

"What is it, Monk? What is it that you want to know?"

Monk looked straight into Peter's face. He wanted to watch Peter as he answered to see if there were any telltale signs, such as a little twitch or blink, to indicate that Peter was lying. "Were you really going to return me, Peter?" Monk asked.

Peter's jaw dropped and his heart sank. Now it was Peter's turn to be speechless, but it wasn't words that Monk was looking for anyway. Words didn't always hold the truth. Monk knew that the truth was often disguised by pretty words. But the tears that began to build up in Peter's eyes told Monk everything he needed to know. Peter had no intention of returning him and Monk knew that now. Words were not necessary, but after what Peter had just done, Monk was not going to stop him from groveling a little. As a matter a fact, he was going to enjoy it.

Regaining his composure, Peter finally spoke. "Oh, Monk, never! I swear, I would never return you. You are my friend, Monk, my best friend in the whole world, and friends don't return friends. Please believe me, I never had any intention of returning you! I should never have done what I did, I know that now. I don't want you to ever doubt me. I love you, Monk!"

Peter's emotional words caught Monk by surprise and he wanted to cry, but he would not. Instead, he climbed up Peter's body and wrapped his arms around his neck, giving him a hug. "I love you, too," said Monk.

This made Peter feel better and worse at the same time.

"Peter, I need to ask you one more thing."

"What's that?" said Peter.

Monk looked at Peter very seriously and said, "It's about the receipt."

Peter's heart sank again. He was hoping that he was forgiven and that they could just stop talking about it. He felt bad enough already and couldn't imagine this was going anywhere good.

"What about the receipt?" Peter cautiously asked.

"I want the receipt, can I have it? You don't need it, Peter. You said yourself that the tighty whities are long gone and you can't return the hat with the sweat stains on it, so can I have it? And I don't mean that nasty hat, I mean the receipt. Can I?"

Peter sighed, feeling relieved. With both hands he removed Monk from his neck and gently set him down on his bed. Peter stood in front of Monk and smiled at him. After all this turmoil, Peter didn't remember what he had done with the receipt for a second, but a quick search of his shirt pocket revealed its location. As an offering of faith, Peter held the receipt out to Monk.

"Do you want to know how I remembered I had this receipt?" Peter said to Monk.

"Okay," Monk answered.

"It was my birthday," Peter began.

Monk wasn't sure what Peter's birthday had to do with what happened today, but he just sat and listened as Peter continued,

"My mom took me shopping and said that I could buy anything in the store that I wanted. As you mentioned earlier, I was looking at everything and then I looked up and there you were. You were everything that I wanted. When we got home that day my mom came into my room and handed me the receipt. She said, 'Peter, you know everyone has to have a birth certificate, and this is Monk's.' Then she told me to make sure I put it in a safe place. I was much shorter at the time so I kept that box hidden in the bottom draw of my dresser. I put all of my important stuff in that box -- I consider it my safe box -- and that is why I put your birth certificate there. I made the connection earlier when we were talking about Captain Paul. I was thinking to myself that wherever he is, I just hope he's safe, and then I thought of the box and the birth certificate."

"So the receipt is actually my birth certificate?" Monk

asked.

"Yes it is, Monk, and if you want it then you should have it."

"Does it have my birth date on it?" Monk asked with anticipation.

Peter smiled and said, "Of course it does. Look." Then, pointing to the date on the receipt, Peter asked, "Do you see it?"

Monk nodded his head yes and started jumping up and down with excitement. "Peter, this is so coooool! I told you it was just meant to be!"

"What are you talking about, Monk?"

"Peter, what are the chances that out of all the animals in the entire world you would pick the one animal that has the exact same birthday as *you*!"

Peter looked at Monk, then at the receipt, and smiled. "Yes," said Peter, "I guess we do share the same birthday, and that *is* cool."

Peter was still holding the birth certificate out for Monk to take and he was surprised when Monk suddenly pushed it away. Confused, Peter asked, "What's wrong?"

"Um," Monk answered, "Peter, who has *your* birth certificate?"

"My mom," said Peter. "She keeps it in the fire safe with all of her important stuff."

Monk thought about that for a moment and then said to Peter, "Then you keep it, Peter. If your mom keeps yours, then you should keep mine."

"Are you sure?"

"Yes, I am," said Monk, smiling. "Put it in a safe place, just like your mom told you to do."

"Okay, Monk, but let's put this in the safe place together." Peter handed Monk the receipt, picked up his box and let Monk tuck the birth certificate safely back inside. Peter put the top back on, secured it with the rubber bands and placed it back on the top shelf in his closet. As he was shutting the door, Monk asked,

"It's safe?"

"Yep, it's safe."

Pirates: Chapter 14

Simple Solution

Antonio sat down on the deck with his hands to his head. "This can't be happening," said Antonio incredulously. "This was an easy job -- take care of the two cooks, set the bottle on the captain's desk and walk away. It couldn't have been any easier. How could anyone mess that up?"

Antonio cringed as he remembered Marcus telling him "it's safe," "don't worry" and "we're family." So much for that! Lifting his head up from his hands for a moment, he said, "Well, Marcus, you said we were going to die. I guess your wish is going to come true. Take a deep breath of that fresh morning air because it will probably be your last."

"Okay, I know it's my fault," said Marcus, "but you don't have to keep rubbing my nose in it. The question now is what are we going to do about it."

"What are we going to do about it? Are there options I'm unaware of, Marcus? I don't know what *you're* going to do about it, but *I* am getting as far away from this island as possible and hoping that Warner never finds me. I suggest that you do the same."

Antonio let it slip again! This boy had him so frazzled that even he was beginning to make mistakes.

"Okay, I thought Warner was a friend of yours. I don't know how friendship works in your world, but in mine we don't kill each other."

"I don't want to talk about Warner. Let's get off the subject."

"We don't have to run away," Marcus offered.

"Yes, we do! By day's end Warner is going to know that we messed up this job and he is going to come looking for me. When he finds me he is going to let me live just long enough to tell him who helped me. Then it will be your turn."

"I'm telling you that we don't have to run. We don't. We can just get another bottle and put it on the desk. No one will know it's not same bottle."

Antonio looked exasperated. "What are you talking about? Marcus, it is not the bottle that's the problem, it is what was *inside* the bottle. That was the purpose of this job, to deliver the message inside the bottle, and the only way you can replace that is if you know what it said." Antonio looked at Marcus, who was stupidly grinning from ear to ear, then said, "Why are you smiling like that?"

"I read the note," said Marcus smugly.

"You read the note," Antonio repeated, clearly dumbfounded. "You touched it. After I told you not to disturb it, you touched it?"

"Yes, I read the note."

"You took it out of the bottle and read it?" said Antonio, still shocked by this revelation.

"I took out the paper, unrolled it and read it," Marcus replied slowly, for effect.

Antonio shook his head in disbelief. "I can't believe you read the note. I should shoot you where you stand, you know. That is a confidential communication between two captains and it is illegal to read it."

"I know," said Marcus, "so shoot me."

Antonio remembered what Captain Warner had said about reading that note and dying. He looked at Marcus now -- Marcus looked fine. It never dawned on him that Warner might be lying.

"How are you feeling?" asked Antonio.

"What, are you a doctor now? I feel fine. Why?"

Antonio started to laugh and gave Marcus a big slap

on the back. In the back of his mind, however, he was still concerned.

"Okay, then," Antonio said, "let's do this and get out of here. Marcus, I will look in the galley to see if I can find a bottle like the one we had. You go to the captain's quarters -- he must have parchment and a quill that you can use to make the note. I'll meet you there."

When Antonio arrived, Marcus was sitting behind the captain's desk holding the new note. "I've got a bottle," said Antonio, holding one up.

The bottle was wider than the original, with a shorter neck, and it was made of amber colored glass.

"It's a good thing that he doesn't know what the original looked like," laughed Marcus.

Sounding annoyed, Antonio remarked, "Marcus, it's the note that matters. The bottle itself is of no significance."

"I am sure you are right, Antonio."

"Let me see the note."

Marcus handed Antonio the note. "Don't let all those fancy words confuse you," Marcus joked, as Antonio read his handiwork.

"Funny," Antonio said, clearly not amused. "Are you sure this is what the note said?"

"I am positive."

Antonio reread the note and wondered what it meant. It didn't seem to make sense to him, and it certainly didn't say anything he would have guessed it would say, but he would probably never know the meaning and just put it out of his mind. He rolled up the note, slid it into the bottle and pressed the cork in as far as it would go. He set the bottle right in the middle of the desk, as Warner had instructed.

Unfortunately, even with the job now done, Marcus and Antonio would have to wait for hours before they could make their escape -- Antonio knew that leaving in the daylight would be impossible without being seen. As they sat there waiting for darkness to come, Antonio reflected on their experience. It had been a long week and Antonio could only hope that their note worked the same as the original would have. He also hoped that he wouldn't have to see Marcus again for a long time. The lad was careless and impulsive. Antonio knew that it wouldn't be long before Marcus missed another of those tiny little details and would have to pay a price.

Pirates: Chapter 15

Ante Up

It started with a slight headache and a pain in his stomach but, over the course of two hours, the abdominal cramps became so bad that he couldn't stand up. He began running a high fever and the sweat was pouring off of him. The tint of his skin was now a pale shade of gray. Marcus lay rolled up in a fetal position on the deck, moaning, as Antonio tried his best to bring down the fever with cool wet rags. Marcus drifted in and out of consciousness throughout the day and was becoming a bit delusional. Antonio kept talking to him, hoping it would keep him in this world, and every now and then Marcus would focus and have a moment of clarity.

"Marcus," said Antonio, "can you hear me?"

"Of course I can hear you, you're yelling in my ear!" Marcus screamed out in pain as he held his stomach. Then, in a barely audible whimper, he said, "Antonio, it hurts, it hurts so bad. Help me . . . please."

"Would you like some water?"

"Don't you have anything stronger?"

"No, Marcus, just water."

"I told you not to drink all the sherry," Marcus said, trying to laugh through the pain.

"Yes, you did."

"Antonio?"

"What, Marcus?"

"This is what it feels like when you eat too many bananas."

Antonio smiled and shook his head, thinking to himself, "Forever the joker." Then Antonio asked again, "Do you want some water?"

"Sure."

Antonio poured some water into Marcus's mouth but he coughed most of it back up.

"I'm sorry, Antonio."

"About what?"

"I forgot about the details."

"It's okay, Marcus."

"Antonio, I'm afraid!" Marcus was shaking.

"I'm here, Marcus, and we are going to get you to a

doctor as soon as we can get out of here. Don't worry."

"I'm not worried for me, Antonio. I am afraid for you."

"Me, why me?"

"Because if I die my mother is never going to forgive you." Just as Marcus finished this sentence, he closed his eyes and stopped talking.

Antonio was gripped by sudden panic. "Marcus, wake up," he said, a look of fear in his eyes. "Please, Marcus, wake up!" It wasn't until he saw Marcus breathing that he relaxed again.

He watched Marcus sleep for more that an hour and in this time he came up with a plan. He knew that the only doctor on the island who he could trust was Doctor Sal, but getting Marcus to him was going to be very difficult. Sal was at the far end of town, a straight walk up the main street, but he would draw far too much attention to himself carrying Marcus. That left him only one other option -- the jungle trail. Traveling along the jungle trail was dangerous enough under normal circumstances, but to attempt it at night, while carrying his sick nephew, Antonio was worried that neither of them would make it to Sal's alive.

As night fell, Antonio scooped Marcus up in his arms and carried him off the ship. Marcus's condition had not improved and Antonio knew that time was of the essence to get him to the doctor. Going through the jungle was going to eat away valuable seconds, but he didn't have a choice. The trail was wide enough to carry Marcus comfortably, but the darkness made moving quickly impossible. Despite Marcus being thin, he was dead weight and it was not easy for a little guy like Antonio to carry him for such a great distance.

After thirty minutes of lumbering along the trail, Antonio was out of breath, his arms ached and his legs felt like they were on fire. He desperately wanted to stop and rest. Rest, in theory, sounded good, but his nephew was dying and the noises coming from the jungle on either side of the trail made him very uneasy. Antonio didn't know what kinds of animals were making the noises, but the thought of becoming dinner for a family of tigers kept him moving. Marcus was still soundly sleeping but his breathing pattern was erratic and had Antonio concerned. Suddenly, Marcus took two unnaturally long, deep breaths. Antonio panicked and began running down the path, hoping not to trip over anything.

"Don't die on me now, lad. *Please* don't die," Antonio pleaded in the darkness.

Pirates: Chapter 16

Sal's Shoes

On the outer edge of town was a building that housed a cobbler shop. The sign over the door read, "Sal's Shoes". It was a red brick building attached at its side to a row of twenty other buildings, all similarly attached, that lined the street. Sal's store had a display window in front decorated nicely with many different styles of men's shoes and boots.

Sal Ferratimo was a retired doctor whose dabbling in shoe design had made him a small fortune. He had begun designing and making his own shoes and boots as a hobby but found that he had a real talent for it. The fact that he loved doing it made it the perfect way for him to spend his retirement.

Sal had been a pirate for more than twenty years and had served as the ship's surgeon on board a notorious pirate vessel for all those years. A few years after leaving the seafaring life, Sal moved to the island with his family and bought the building that now was his cobbler shop. He renovated it, opened shop and quickly turned it into a reputable men's shoe business. But it wasn't until Sal began designing and making women's shoes that the business really took off. He had started shipping them to stores on the mainland because many more women lived there than on the island and that's when his ladies' shoe line caught on like wild fire. It wasn't long afterward that this simple retired pirate had the aristocratic women all over Europe abuzz.

Now, for obvious reasons, Dr. Sal's fame and fortune are just a few of the secrets that he has to keep hidden from his friends as well as his fans. He lives a simple life out on the island and mostly keeps to himself. In the pirate world he is still known just as good old Sal, a retired doctor who likes to work on shoes, but in the fashion world, just the mention of his name -- Ferratimo -- can send women's heartrates racing through the roof.

Despite Sal's desire to leave the pirate life behind, and despite the fact that his love for shoes had made him a successful and weathy man, he hadn't been able to just walk away from being a doctor. Helping people was something he felt proud to be able to do, so he had a private entrance put in at the back of his building that led into a small office. The entrance could not be seen from the street so his patients could come and go without being seen.

Sal was in the middle of finishing up a special shoe design for some prissy princess when he heard a banging at the back door. Antonio was knocking frantically, hoping that Dr. Sal was home.

"I'm coming, I'm coming. Stop pounding on the door already," Sal yelled.

Antonio could hear Sal's voice coming from inside the house and the door opened. Sal stood in the doorway and immediately focused on the unconscious man in Antonio's arms. He quickly looked around to see if anyone else was nearby then said, "Come in, quickly!"

Sal instantly shut the door behind them as Antonio stepped into the house. He was rather pale himself and dripping with sweat.

"Antonio, what's going on? What happened to this boy?" Sal asked.

Breathing heavily, Antonio said, "I'm not sure, but I think it may be some kind of poison."

"What makes you think that?"

Antonio hesitated. That question put Antonio into a bad spot -- he needed to keep Warner out of this conversation but wasn't sure how to go about it. "Sal, I can't tell you exactly why, but let's say I am almost sure."

Calmly, Sal responded, "Antonio, you know that I am discreet -- I have lived in your world before. If you want me to help this boy I need to know what you know. There are hundreds of different kinds of poisons and they are all treated differently, and your friend here looks like he is running out of time."

Antonio took a deep breath, still unsure about exactly what he could say. "Sal, let's just say there was a piece of parchment paper intended for only one person to receive and my nephew handled it. Now he is very sick and I can't come up with any other reason why. Does that help?"

"So you think that the poison was somehow on or in the parchment?"

"Yes, that is exactly what I'm saying."

Sal's expression instantly changed to one of extreme concern and he hoped that Antonio hadn't noticed. Sal had a feeling that he knew exactly what the poison was and, if he was right, it might already be too late for him to help. Based on the condition of this boy, the point of no return may have already passed.

"Antonio, set him down on the cot in the corner," Sal said, pointing. "I am going to give him a few antidotes which might help him but I can't promise you anything."

"I understand," Antonio answered.

"If he has been poisoned with what I'm thinking, there is only a small chance that I can save him at this stage. He is obviously a strong boy and a fighter so we can only hope he keeps up that fight. He is very lucky for your insight, Antonio, because it is unlikely that any doctor would have realized it was poison until after he was dead."

Antonio recalled what Warner had said about emotions and being able to separate yourself from them and he realized that Warner was right. He should never have involved Marcus. Even if he had not been close to his nephew, there was a shared history between them. Marcus was part of his family and now, if Marcus didn't pull through, he would have to live with the consequences. Antonio thought about mass and confession and knew that no act of contrition was going to make this right. All he could do was hope for Marcus's survival.

Antonio's thoughts continued to weigh on his mind while Sal worked on Marcus. He reflected that even if he had chosen someone other than Marcus to assist him with this job, someone who he didn't have any connection to, that he still would be feeling bad if something like this had happened. Antonio's compassion for people was real and it struck him suddenly that maybe he just didn't belong in this pirate world either.

He would decide what to do about that another day -- at the moment he had a job to do, and that was to help

Marcus fight. As he walked towards the cot where Marcus lay, Antonio looked across the room and noticed a small table. On the table, right in the center, was a white doily with a bowl of fruit on top. There were apples and oranges, but it was the bananas that brought him back to the bottle, the bottle that Warner had given him. The monkey had it now and he couldn't help but wonder what he was doing with it at that moment.

Pirates:
Chapter 17

The Note

Monk climbed up the front of Peter's body and was hanging from his shoulder with his feet at his hip. With the receipt tucked securely back in the box, Monk was feeling really good about the day. Peter loved him, he had an official birth certificate and, to top it all off, Peter and Monk shared the same birthday. With all of the good things that had come out of the day, he knew he should simply enjoy the moment. But, Monk being Monk, he had just one more button to push.

"Pete, can I tell you something that I just remembered?"

"Sure, Monk, what is it?"

"It's just something that you might want to keep in

mind for the future."

"What do I need to keep in mind?" asked Peter.

Abruptly, Monk swung from Peter's arm onto the bed, ran across the covers and opened the top drawer of Peter's nightstand. Monk pulled out a notepad and a pen, then shut the drawer. He sat down at the edge of the bed and started writing.

Peter watched him for a moment then, somewhat confused, asked, "Monk, I thought you had something you wanted to tell me?"

"I do, Peter, but I want you to remember it so I am writing it down. After you read it you can put it in your safe box."

Monk continued to scribble away for a minute and, when he was done, he tore the paper from the pad and set the pad and pen on the bed. Monk then bounced across the bed and handed Peter the paper.

"Peter, read it out loud, please."

"Okay," Peter replied, a little skeptically, then read aloud, "For future reference, the Bon Ton has a strict thirty day return policy. A store credit will be issued after that and no returns whatsoever are accepted after sixty days from purchase date. Sale items are final and can not be returned at any time."

As Peter finished reading the note, Monk started to giggle. Monk had known all along that he couldn't be returned all these years later, but he wanted to make sure that *Peter* knew that *he* knew that returning him was never an option to begin with.

Peter looked intently at Monk, as if to say, "What is *this* for?" but suddenly Monk found it all too funny to bear. The more he thought about the note and the expression on Peter's face as he read it, the funnier it was, and Monk started laughing so hard he couldn't sit up any longer. He was now rolling around on Peter's bed laughing and pounding his hands on the quilt. He was laughing so hard he could hardly catch his breath.

"Peter, you should see your face," Monk howled with laughter. "Ha, ha, ha, ha, ha . . . I can't breathe! Peter (gasp), Pete, please . . . stop looking at me like that. You're killing me!"

Monk was hysterically laughing and Peter could do nothing but continue to stare at him. Peter did not want to find any humor in the note so he had on his best poker face and kept shaking his head in disbelief, but Peter could not keep it inside much longer. As he fought every urge not to give in to Monk's laughter, he couldn't help but be impressed by how smart Monk had gotten over the years. Oh, sure, Monk had a long way to go before he was some rocket scientist (or even a 7th grader for that matter!), but Monk's little note did show Peter that he was going to have to work harder in the future to pull one over on him.

Monk's laughter finally reached the contagious level

and Peter couldn't continue to hold back. He started with a little chuckle and worked his way into a full belly laugh with tears streaming down his face. Peter, too, was now rolling around on the bed, he and Monk both in an uncontrollable state of hysterics, when Monk managed to stop laughing just long enough to say,

"You know, I'm just looking out for you, Peter. I would hate to see you get stuck having to wear tighty whities that pinch you when you walk."

Monk's and Peter's howling hit a fever pitch and it seemed they might possibly die laughing. But, slowly, their fits and bursts of laughter started to subside and the two of them finally pooped out and lay silently on Peter's bed, just staring at the ceiling. Monk continued to smile, very happy as he recalled once again the events of the day. They remained like this for a few minutes when Peter finally broke the silence.

"Where do you think Captain Paul is?" Peter asked.

"I really don't know," Monk answered in earnest.

"Monk, what do you think about us cracking open that bottle and seeing what the note says?"

"I think it's a good idea, Peter, but don't you think it would be better to simply pop the cork and slide the note out? I don't think your mom would like it if we got little pieces of glass all over the place."

Peter laughed and said, "Cracking open the bottle is just a figure of speech, Monk."

"I don't know what that means, Peter, but I still think popping the cork is a better idea -- no mess. You know how your mom is."

Peter, rolling his eyes, thought to himself, "Smart, yes, but yet so far to go," then said to Monk, "Okay, Monk, we'll do it your way. Let's pop that cork and see what the note says."

Monk took the bottle with one hand, raised it to his lips and, gripping the cork with his teeth, gave it a tug. As Monk pulled and twisted, the cork slowly eased out of the bottle and then they heard a *POP*.

Peter reached over and took the cork from Monk's mouth while saying, "Okay, Monk, see if you can slide that note out."

Monk turned the bottle upside down and the note fell into the neck. He then tapped the bottom of the bottle with the palm of his hand and the note slid out just enough for Peter to pinch it with two fingers and pull it out.

"I've got it!" Peter said with great excitement.

"Unroll it, Peter. Hurry!" Monk urged, as if the note would vanish before they could read it.

They were both anxious with anticipation. Peter unrolled the paper and couldn't believe what he was reading. He read it once over in his head and tried to figure it out. Impatiently, Monk interrupted Peter's thoughts.

"Peter, tell me, what does it say?"

Pirates: Chapter 18

Word

Warner was in his quarters when there came a knock at the door. It was 8 a.m. and he was never supposed to be bothered before 8:30. Warner, obviously annoyed by this disruption, yelled,

"Who is knocking at this hour? I will have you swabbing the decks for this!"

First Mate Pantuzzo knew that bothering the captain this early was not in his best interests but he had weighed that against the importance of the information that he had just received. If the captain considered it nonessential or trivial then he would be swabbing decks and washing dishes.

"It's First Mate Pantuzzo, sir."

Knowing that Pantuzzo was not usually one to bother him for no good reason, Warner's tone lost some of its edge. "Come in and tell me what is so important that it couldn't wait a half an hour."

"It's about Captain Delham, sir."

Warner became excited and instantly his attitude changed. He was now fully alert and very interested in what Panntuzzo had to say. Impatiently he beckoned, "Don't just stand out there, come in already!"

It was early but Pantuzzo was dressed and ready for business, unlike the captain who looked like he had just crawled out of bed.

"What is it, is he dead?" Warner excitedly asked.

"I don't know yet, sir."

Without giving Pantuzzo a chance to continue, the captain, with fire in his eyes, snapped, "You disturbed me to tell me you don't know if he is dead?"

"No, sir."

"Then why are you here?"

"We have word that Captain Delham returned to the ship yesterday along with sailor Nic Meloni."

"Who is he?"

"He is a she, sir, and she is their lookout. The information is still coming in but at the moment we know that Meloni left the ship and returned with Marten Centeni, the ship's doctor."

"Have we heard from Antonio yet?"

"No, sir, we haven't," said Pantuzzo.

"So how do we know that he did what I asked? How do we know he didn't just take my money and run for the hills?"

"We don't, sir, but we do know, from a good source, that the doctor has sent Meloni into town in search of an antidote for poison. A specific poison, sir."

Warner was looking at Pantuzzo with an expression that bordered on begging, wanting to hear only one thing at this point. "Is it our poison?" he asked. "Tell me they are looking for a cure for our poison."

"Yes, sir, they are."

The truth was that Pantuzzo didn't really know, but he wasn't going to tell the captain this. In his mind it didn't really matter -- if the girl was sent to look for the antidote to a poison, Delham was poisoned.

The captain began to smile and then, laughing, said, "We have him!" Banging both hands on his desk in victory, he continued, "I got you, Delham! I got you and you will suffer. Mr. Pantuzzo, we will celebrate but, first, we need to make sure that the lookout, Ms. Meloni, does not return with a possible antidote. There are only three places she can get what she is looking for. I want you to post two men at each location to pick her up."

"But, sir, why risk being tied to this in any way? Delham has been sick for hours now and that poison should be at a point where medicine won't help him. He

134

is going to die, so why capture her?"

"Mario," said Warner.

Pantuzzo was surprised and concerned to hear his first name. The captain never referred to him in this way.

"I have been waiting for years for this moment and I want Delham to look into the eyes of death with no chance of hope," Warner said coldly. "The girl will not return with a cure, do you understand me?"

There was no mistaking Warner's tone or the icy cold look in his eyes -- this was a direct order and there would be no argument.

"Yes, sir. I will do as you ask."

"Very good, Mr. Pantuzzo!"

"Thank you, sir," Pantuzzo answered as he left the room.

Pantuzzo summoned six men and gave them their assignments in pairs. He instructed them that Meloni was to be brought back to the ship unharmed and that they should not speak to her or offer any information about where they were taking her. He also had to alert his source because he needed them to provide someone at each of the three locations who would recognize her for Warner's men. As Pantuzzo was setting Warner's plan in motion, it crossed his mind that Delham's lookout could have already gotten the medicine and returned to the ship, but he was not crazy enough to mention that to Captain Warner.

Pirates: Chapter 19

Poison

Nic had been to Dr. Sal's shop many times before, but she wasn't used to going the long way and she knew that there wasn't much time left for her to get there. Word was sent out to the entire crew that an emergency call of duty was enacted and that they had two hours to return to the ship. She made her way through the jungle as quickly as she could, trying to focus only on the task at hand, but her mind wandered as she walked -- she thought about Monk, about the poisoned bottle and about Peter.

Dr. Sal's house was somewhat visible from the tree line of the jungle and Nic hurried toward it as soon as she caught a glimpse of it. She knew that the back door could not be seen from the street but still she ran quickly to avoid being noticed. Nic knocked twice, then once and then twice more, a signal that let Sal know that someone from Captain Paul's ship was at the door. Sal recognized the knock instantly and answered the door without hesitation.

"Come in, Nic! A nice surprise, you coming here. I see you are still wearing those awful boots. I have a pair of shoes that would look marvelous on you. You're such a pretty girl, why do you dress like a boy?"

Nic just smiled in response. She could see that Sal had two patients in his office and the one on the cot didn't look so good. She nodded at Sal and then walked from the door into Sal's cutting room. Sal followed her.

The smell of leather filled the room and, as Nic looked around, she could see ten different shades of black and brown leather hanging from the walls. Dr. Sal also had rolls of textured material that were about three feet high standing upright along the length of one entire wall. The materials seemed like they'd be soft to the touch and came in a variety of pretty colors. Nic imagined that Sal must use these for the women's shoes he makes. The two tables in the room were each big enough for someone to sleep on and there were scissors and knives hanging from the front edge of each table. Nic stopped near the tables and turned to look at Sal, who had stopped also. She remembered that she had liked Dr. Sal instantly the first time she met him. She had been sick with a bad case of swamp fever and Dr. Sal had nursed her back to health. He was such a kind man that Nic found it hard to believe that he was ever a pirate.

"Hi, Sal," Nic said at last.

"It's nice to see you, Nic. I was serious about the shoes, you know."

"I know you were, but I like my boots."

"You know what, then? I am going to make you the most beautiful pair of pirate boots you have ever seen."

"As long as they are comfortable and I can climb in them, I would like that. Thank you." Nic smiled. "And, Dr. Sal?"

"What, Nic?"

"No heels please."

Sal laughed. "Nic, I would never put heels on pirate boots. Now, tell me why you're here."

Nic's expression turned serious as she said, "I need to talk to you about poisons and antidotes."

"Poisons?" Dr. Sal asked nervously, then, putting a finger to his lips, he whispered, "Shhh."

Sal turned around and looked into the other room. He saw that Antonio was now asleep in the chair next to his friend, Marcus. Sal quietly walked over to the door between the rooms and gently shut it.

Pirates: Chapter 20

Standing Watch

Nic came out of Sal's cutting room looking nervous and a bit pale. The news she got from Dr. Sal about the poison was not good and she was anxious to get back to the ship. As Dr. Sal started leading her back through his office, Nic noticed that the two patients were both sleeping and spoke in a hushed voice,

"Dr. Sal, I need to go out your front door."

"But, Nic, you didn't come in the front door."

"I know, but I have to go out the front."

"It could be risky," Sal cautioned.

"I know that but I have to go out the front. It's important."

Dr. Sal thought about it momentarily and said, "What if someone sees you going out and knows you didn't come in that way? There would be questions asked. The men who run this island have eyes everywhere, you know."

"I know, but I have to risk it. Maybe you can tell them that I'm your niece and that I have been visiting for a few days."

"It won't work."

"Why?" asked Nic, surprised at his quick response.

"Because my niece would not be caught dead in those boots." Dr. Sal started to laugh.

"Ha, ha, ha," Nic smiled and pretended to laugh.

Then Sal said, "Okay, you can be my niece, but you have to promise me that if you are going to continue to dress like that you won't tell anyone that we're related."

This made Nic laugh for real. "I'll tell you what, *Uncle Sal*, if you give me that leather satchel you have on the counter, I can put all of my things in it and then if anyone questions why I was here we can say that you invited me here for my birthday so you could give me the satchel."

Dr. Sal looked confused and asked, "Why would I do that?"

Now Nic looked confused. She explained, "It's my birthday, so the satchel is a present from you to me for my birthday."

"It is?"

"Yes," said Nic, "I think that works."

"Is it really your birthday?" asked Sal.

Nic smiled and rolled her eyes. "No, silly! This is just what we are going to tell them, that it is my birthday. This is only *if* anyone asks."

Dr. Sal liked Nic very much and was thankful that she was not his niece because he knew that he would have a tough time ever saying no to her. He asked her,

"You like that satchel, don't you?"

"Um, yes. It's very nice."

"You don't have any money to actually buy it, though, do you?"

"No, I don't. But, please, Dr. Sal. I'm only trying to protect both of us since you think someone will see me leaving out the front."

"Okay, you can pay me later for the satchel. I will still make you the boots for free. No heels."

"Right," said Nic, "no heels."

Nic gave Sal a hug then went to work moving the contents of her old bag to the new one. She handed the old bag to Dr. Sal and walked to the front door.

"Nic," said Sal as she opened the door.

"What?"

"You're such a pretty girl. Why do you dress like a boy?"

"Bye, Uncle Sal," she giggled, as she walked out the

front door.

Nic was zigzagging her way through the crowded streets as fast as she could without calling attention to herself. She knew that going through town would get her back to the ship in time and she was excited. She was thinking about Peter and the poisoned note when, as she turned a corner, she was grabbed from behind. Nic started to scream but the man had put his hand over her mouth and dragged her down an alley. Nic was kicking and thrashing about and her right foot managed to catch the attacker in the knee. She could hear him grunt in pain and then he dropped her. As Nic fell from his grasp she landed on top of the leather satchel and she could hear glass crunching inside the bag. "The bottles," she thought to herself, "not the bottles!" She managed to get to her feet and could hear someone calling her name from the street. Nic turned towards the voice and locked eyes for a second with Matais. He could see that she was in need of help but before he crossed the street she was thrown into a burlap sack and dragged away by two very large thugs.

When Matais finally got to the alley Nic was nowhere to be seen. He stood at the entrance to the alley for a few minutes, then turned and ran down the street, trying his best not to knock anyone over as he raced back to the ship.

142

Pirates:
Chapter 21

A Friend Betrayed

Peter hadn't answered Monk about what the note said, so Monk pulled down on Peter's hands to try to see it himself. That didn't work, since Peter was gripping the parchment rather tightly, but finally, at Monk's insistence, Peter began to read the note out loud:

Dearest Peter,

We will be setting sail in 3 hours and Monk has instructions that need to be followed. I have prepared a list of things that you will be required to do once we return from our voyage. I hope there will be no hard feelings.

For Future Reference --

Trust is like a grain of sand and it is very hard to get back once it's lost. It must be cherished and tucked away in a safe place.

On your return to the ship you must bring:
1 pair of used magic pirate boots
  (no substitutes)
1 pair of handmade magic wrist bands

Also, here is your punishment for breaking the destruction clause to Rule #1702. You will complete this upon our return:

Swab the decks	Clean galley
Clean trash barrels	Clean the mess hall
Wash all pots & pans	Clean all linens
Clean Captain's quarters	
Polish Captain's boots	

Your Trusted Friend & Captain,

When Peter finished reading the note to Monk he dropped it onto the bed. The words had hit Peter hard. He was hurt, he was angry and he felt a sense of, as he put it quite loudly, "*Betrayal!!!*"

Peter glared at Monk and continued screaming, "You, who call yourself my friend . . . you betrayed me! You gave me up, you turned me in. I know everyone has a price, Monk, so what did I go for? A dozen bananas? Maybe less?"

Peter took two deep breaths, trying to control his temper, but he just couldn't do it. He continued, "'For future reference'-- I wonder where I have read that before?"

"Peter, it wasn't like that," Monk interrupted.

"Oh, it wasn't like that? So you admit it was you who betrayed me?" Peter said, shaking his head in disgust.

"I had to, Peter. I didn't have any choice."

Peter was seething. "We all have choices, Monk. Like, throwing you out my bedroom window, that would be a choice."

"Not a very good choice," said Monk, sounding a little nervous.

Peter started chasing Monk around the room -- over the bed, under the bed, from side to side -- and then Monk climbed up the open bedroom door and sat on the top of it.

"Peter, please stop before you hurt someone!" Monk pleaded.

"Who would that someone be, Monk? You?" Peter panted.

"Yes!"

Peter grabbed the door and swung it hard. Monk lost his balance and fell from the top. Then Peter started the chase all over again.

"I am going to get you, Monk! You wait and see, it is only a matter of time."

"Peter, you sound a little winded. You should really start doing more cardiovascular exercise -- the treadmill, the stairmaster, and I hear run-walking is fun. You do know that exercise is the key to having a healthy heart."

"Well, I guess you won't have to worry about that since we all know you don't *have* a heart, because if you did you wouldn't have . . . betrayed meeeeeeeee!"

Peter leaped over the bed to tackle Monk, but he missed. He sat on the floor trying to catch his breath. After a few minutes, with Monk watching him warily from the window sill, Peter spoke softly,

"Monk, you hurt me."

"Like threatening to return me to the Bon Ton kind of hurt?" Monk asked pointedly.

"Oh, now you're going to bring that up? Is that how it's going to be from now on -- every time we disagree or argue you'll throw the Bon Ton in my face?"

"Well you did it, Peter, and I don't think I did anything to deserve that," said Monk.

"I said I was sorry and, as I recall, you said you forgave me."

"I do. And, for this, I think you need to just sit there for a second and let me explain what happened. Then if you want to hate me, fine, but at least you will hate me knowing the full story."

Peter stayed sitting on the floor with his back against the wall, and Monk sat on the bed, ready to leap to safety if he had to.

Pirates: Chapter 22

The Explanation

"Okay, I'm not really sure where to start," began Monk.

"I know where you can start," offered Peter.

"Where?"

"You were gone for seven days. What did you do on the ship for seven days?"

"I didn't really do anything. Most of the time I sat in the crow's nest looking down at the ship and out at the dock. I thought that was the best place to see the captain coming, before he would see me."

"Obviously that didn't work out so good, did it?" Peter said sarcastically.

"Peter, let me finish before you judge. When I first

got there I just thought that everyone was away. But there were a few times that I thought that I heard whispering. It got creepy, so I climbed up into the crow's nest and stayed up there for the entire seven days."

"Is that your explanation? Your justification? What, were you mad at me for sending you? If you didn't want to go you should have just said so."

"Peter, don't start up again, I am not done."

"Well . . . go ahead, then," Peter said impatiently.

"I told you that I thought I heard voices . . ."

"Well that's not a surprise, really," interrupted Peter.

Monk glared at Peter, then continued, "At first I thought it was Stanley and Melvin, but they never came out of the galley. For seven days, they never came out of the galley. Who does that? They didn't even come out to go to the bathroom. Now, don't you find that a bit odd?"

That caught Peter's attention. He was starting to find Monk's story intriguing. Monk continued,

"So I sat up in the lookout until Sunday morning and I was almost sure that I saw the galley door open a crack -- and you know that door never stays open on its own -- so I got a little scared and I thought it was a good idea to get out of there. I started to leave and as I walked past the bottle, which was on the deck the whole time I was there, as I had told you, it dawned on me that whoever was in the galley wasn't coming out because they were waiting for me to leave because they wanted that bottle. Why else would anyone hide out in the galley for seven days? So I made it look like I was leaving and I stood on the gangplank, but then I turned suddenly, ran back over to the bottle, put it in my satchel and then took off."

When Monk paused for a second, Peter questioned, "Monk, how do you know anyone was even on the ship? Maybe it was all in your head."

Monk shook his head as he answered, "I didn't leave the ship. I went just far enough down the plank that I could leap to the rail. I shimmied along the rail to the front of the ship and I climbed back on and hid where I could see the galley and watch."

"So, did Stanley and Melvin come out and say, 'Thank God the monkey's gone?'"

"Ha, ha, ha," Monk said, his sarcastic tone matching Peter's. "No, it was not Stanley or Melvin. But two men did come out and they were not very happy that the bottle was gone. As a matter of fact, the bottle was the reason they were on the ship."

Peter could not believe what he was hearing but this would be a lie way too big for Monk to come up with.

"Why did they want the bottle?" Peter asked.

"They were supposed to put the bottle with the note on the captain's desk and leave."

"But you took the bottle," Peter said, starting to laugh, "so what happened?"

"Antonio went and got a bottle from the galley and Marcus said he knew what was written on the note so he went into the captain's quarters and wrote a new note."

"So, you even got their names?"

"Yep," Monk said proudly.

"Pretty good. And then, after they wrote the note, did they leave?"

"No, and that is where the story gets scary because Marcus started to get really sick and it looked like he was going to die. A couple of times I thought he did die, that is how bad he looked. When it got dark, Antonio carried him off of the ship."

"What did he get sick from?" Peter asked.

"Well, before Marcus got sick, Antonio said something about touching the note."

"What did he say?"

"When he first found out that Marcus had read the note he said, 'You touched the note,' like he couldn't believe it. Then again, later, he said, 'I can't believe you touched it' and asked him if he was feeling okay, and that was before Marcus started to get sick."

"Wow! That is such a great story!" Peter said excitedly.

"Peter, I think you are missing the point."

"What point?"

"The note made Marcus sick, like dying sick, and they were supposed to put that note on Captain Paul's desk.

151

He was the one who was supposed to take the note out of the bottle, Peter. *He* would have been the one who got sick."

Peter's eyes grew wide. He realized now that he had been right, in a way, in thinking that Captain Paul was in danger. Peter was both excited about this and troubled.

"Monk, I was right! When I decided to send you to the ship, I was right -- the captain was in trouble. If I hadn't sent you there he would have opened that bottle. Monk, we have to tell the captain," Peter declared.

"I already told the captain," said Monk.

Peter gave Monk an all-knowing look, nodded his head and said, "You took all the credit didn't you? Why else would he punish me if I saved his life. You took the credit and I get to scrub the decks. Monk, you wouldn't have been on the ship to see the men if it weren't for me."

"Peter, I assure you that the captain knows it was you who saved him. But you did pretend to burn the boots, you were the one who broke the rule, and that is what you are getting punished for. Now, if you are done feeling sorry for yourself, we need to get back to the ship, unless you still feel the need to throw me out the window."

Peter sighed. "Sorry about that, Monk, and you were right."

"Thank you, Peter."

"And, you know, I think I do need to do more cardio," Peter laughed. "That chase wore me out. But, Monk, I forgot to ask, how did you find the captain?"

"Let's go and I'll tell you on the way."

Peter had been waiting anxiously for five weeks to get asked back to the ship but, now that he was going, he was nervous and no longer looking forward to it.

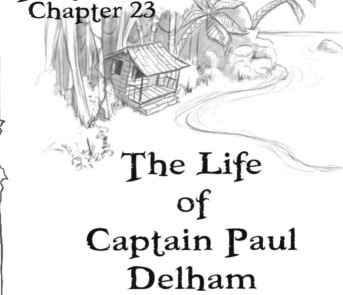

Pirates:
Chapter 23

The Life
of
Captain Paul
Delham

Paul Delham walked along the shore with the waves breaking and the water washing up over his feet. The ocean water was cold and it made his feet tingle but he knew that later, during the heat of the day, the same water would feel refreshing. The reef where he was walking was such a beautiful part of the island and no one but Paul knew that it even existed. The people who came to this island didn't care about sandy beaches or the surf -- they were pirates and they came here to get away from the sea. When they came ashore it was time for them to eat, drink and be merry, and if there was any time leftover, some of them tried to catch up on sleep. But Paul didn't want any part of the town; it wasn't his thing and, even if it was, it wasn't safe for a man of his stature to be wondering through the streets of that town anyway.

Paul found the solitude of the reef comforting, and walking along the beach in the morning cleared his head. He would walk as far as Starry Cove, a secluded area set back into the jungle that had the most beautiful waterfall in the world. The water coming over the falls was so clear that it sparkled and glinted in the sun. It reminded Paul of a constellation of stars which is why he named it Starry Cove. He would then walk back down the beach and sit in the sand, listening to the birds chirping and the waves crashing against the shore. He loved to watch the sunrise from here; no matter what the day ahead might bring, for Paul, it always started perfectly on the reef.

The reef was Paul's secret home away from the ship, but he had realized long ago that someone needed to know of his whereabouts just in case a problem arose in his absence. Paul had gone to his friend Stanley, who was so honored to be entrusted with such a big secret that he had helped Paul devise a way to get off and on the ship without being seen. To do this successfully, Paul would anchor the Rising Sea in the very last slip at the end of the dock, and he would always bring the ship in at night -- this way he could disappear during the chaos of the crew getting ready for leave. He would set off on foot in the dark and, by the time Stanley had the crew ready to go into town for their leave, Paul would be halfway to the reef and no one was the wiser.

Paul closed his eyes and felt the morning sun's warmth on his face. As the breeze gently blew through his hair, the smell of the sea air was fresh and invigorating and he could hear the seagulls squawking as they dove into the water in search of breakfast. Paul found it hard to believe that on an island filled with thieves and killers he could still be so close to heaven. Of course, even in heaven, he had thought out a definitive escape strategy.

Paul had all that he needed to live comfortably in his own little paradise. In the years that he had been coming here he had managed to build himself a small house. It was made primarily out of bamboo and giant palm fronds, and it was nestled just inside the tree line, at the edge of the jungle, so it couldn't be seen from the water. Inside he had only a few pieces of furniture: there was a bed, covered with blankets and a pillow that Paul had taken from the ship, a table with a small oil lamp on it and two matching chairs. Paul had made the bed, table and chairs himself, out of bamboo, and they were a little primitive, but perfectly functional. Overall, it was a very comfortable place and it felt safer than being on the ship.

Whenever Paul would stay at his island home he lived off the land, for the most part, by fishing and eating fruits, nuts and coconuts from the nearby trees and bushes. He had plenty of fresh drinking water available from the cove. But, even though he liked to provide for himself in this way, Stanley, who always watched over him like a mother hen, would not let Paul leave the ship without a care package filled with, among other things, meats, breads, cookies and jams. Stanley was a good friend and, even though Paul knew that the crew saw him just as the goofy cook, Paul liked him and knew he could be trusted. If Stanley were taken prisoner, Paul was sure that no one would interrogate him for vital information. Unless the captors were looking for Stanley's famous apple pie recipe that had been in his family for generations, Paul was confident that no one would question Stanley at all. In Paul's mind, no one could be trusted more with knowing his whereabouts than Stanley. So when Paul saw Monk bounding down the beach towards him, he knew something was wrong.

Monk was excited and scared and talking so fast that Paul was finding it hard to follow him. Paul had to stop him several times to try to get him to slow down and repeat what Paul had missed. It took a while, but eventually Monk had Paul updated on everything that had happened in the last seven days on the ship, and then some. Monk was a wealth of information -- he remembered names and described each of the men; he told of freeing Melvin and Stanley, who had been held

157

captive in the galley for the entire week; he explained how Stanley was in no shape to come looking for the captain himself so he had had no choice but to tell Monk where to find him. According to Monk, Melvin was hit so hard on the head that he only regained consciousness when Monk had found them and Stanley was now nursing him back to health. Monk had also brought Paul both of the bottles from the ship -- the original and the one Antonio and Marcus had created -- with the poison bottle wrapped in a small sack so that Monk wouldn't confuse the two. The captain's head was spinning with all of this information. He felt his safe little world crashing down around him. Paul walked with Monk back to his house and shortly after Monk finished his story, Paul sent him back to Peter's with written instructions.

Paul stood in the entrance to his hut staring out at the sea. In one hand he held the bottle with the poisoned note still inside and in the other was the forged note that the man named Marcus had made. The words on the note opened old wounds and memories that he had long ago hidden away:

> There is no return from where
> you are going!
> I will soon have what you don't.

Paul knew exactly what the first part of the note meant, but it was the second sentence that was haunting. The words were a reminder of why he became a pirate so many years ago: family. Paul thought about how he had chosen this life because of his family, then shook his head in disgust. At one time he had been a full-time father and husband. He had inherited half of his father's land and one of the three houses the family had owned. There were twenty men, nine women and fourteen children who lived in housing on the property who helped Paul keep the orchard running from day to day. Paul considered each and every one of those people part of his family and when there was a holiday, a birthday or a new baby, they would all celebrate as one.

"Family," Paul said to himself. He had become a pirate to save his family. The Ring of Hope had a long tainted history of people who had lived on the run while savage pirates gave chase trying to get the ring from them. But Paul's father had worn it a lifetime with no such problems, and Paul had worn it for nearly five years without incident . . . but then, one summer evening, the chase began.

Paul closed his eyes and tried to remember that day. It was July. Normally it would have been hot and humid in July but the week had been atypically mild -- no more than seventy degrees each day with the nights dropping slightly into the sixties. It was a Friday and the day had been possibly one of the nicest of the summer. Dinner with Kate and the kids had been entertaining -- his son had been having one of his "Why, Daddy" moments (why-does-that-work-like-that and why-do-people-do-this), peppering Paul with a million questions and never being satisfied with the answers, while his daughter had more pressing matters to talk about -- she was getting a new kitten and the list of names she had compiled had to be gone over as a family (it was decided that Tilly was everyone's favorite). Life was perfect, the summer had been perfect. Paul had gone to bed a rich man in so many ways . . . but had woken up desperate and nearly dead.

Paul remembered hearing Charlotte, the housekeeper, screaming, "Mr. Delham! Mr. Delham! Raiders! Raiders in the house!" Raiders was what Charlotte called pirates and that was all the warning Paul got. As he started to climb out of bed the door burst open, Kate screamed and he looked up into the intruder's eyes. He remembered thinking that the eyes were so black and lifeless that they must belong to a person with no soul. Then came the sound of an explosion, a shooting pain in his chest and darkness. When Paul regained consciousness, he was lying on the bedroom floor between the bed and the night table. His chest hurt like crazy and his head ached like he had been kicked by a mule. Then he remembered Kate's scream and the dead black eyes and Paul started to panic. He managed to get to his feet by supporting his weight on the nightstand but it was hard to walk, his vision was hazy, and he stumbled around the room, almost falling twice. He noticed blood on his hands and his ring -- his father's ring! -- was gone. He called out for Kate but she didn't answer. Paul saw a chair against the wall and used it to support himself as he moved around the room looking for Kate, but she wasn't there. As he turned to go out of the room he saw a piece of paper crumpled up into a ball near the door. He reached down for it and almost fell over, again, but the chair kept him from tumbling onto the floor. As he stood up with the note his head was pounding like a drum. Paul opened up the paper and his heart sank when he read the words:

I now have what you don't.

Paul called out for help as loud as he could but no one came. He moved slowly and painfully down the hall into his daughter's room -- the bed was empty and the covers were in a pile on the floor. No one was there. He could see across the hall into his boy's room and he, too, was gone. Paul stumbled down the hallway into the bathroom. Looking into the mirror Paul could see that his white cotton shirt was stained almost completely red with a hole up between his shirt collar and shoulder. His hair was matted down with dried blood and, after examining his head, he discovered a cut on his scalp that was just deep enough to cause a great deal of bleeding. Paul's hands were shaking as he unbuttoned his shirt. Some of the blood on his chest had already dried, causing the shirt to stick to his skin and making its removal more painful than it should have been. Once his shirt was off, Paul stared at his chest in the mirror and he could see a small hole in the upper part of his chest, close to his collar bone. When he turned just slightly sideways he could see a second hole, this one in his back in the same area as the one in the front. The holes had already started to scab over and blood was crusted around them. From a bucket next to the sink he transferred water into the basin with a large wooden ladle. As he rinsed the blood from his hands he noticed his ring and paused. His head was still groggy, but he was sure that it hadn't been on his hand when he regained consciousness . . . "Or was it?" he thought. Now he wasn't sure. When he finished rinsing his hands the basin water was bright red. Paul wanted to clean his chest but couldn't find the strength to empty and refill the basin so, instead, he dipped the only unstained part of his shirt directly into the bucket and proceeded to clean off the wound.

A feeling of lightheadedness washed over Paul for a second -- he lost his footing and stumbled backwards, coming to rest against the wall. Paul closed his eyes. He thought of the note and of his family and his knees buckled under his weight, his body slowly sliding down the wall until he was sitting on the floor. He let himself fall sideways and his head and shoulder gently came to a stop against the adjoining wall. He opened his eyes and a shimmering light caught his attention. Paul sat straight up and saw the light was radiating from his hand, from the gold band. He twisted the ring around his knuckle until it came off and examined it. His eyes locked on the inscription and Paul read the words out loud, "To all that need hope." In his head all he could think about was Kate and the kids. If anyone needed hope, they did.

Paul had not read the inscription on the ring in years and, in all the time he had owned it, he had only read it out loud once -- the day his mother had given it to him. His mother was so sure this was The Ring of Hope that she was willing to bet everything she had on it with no proof, just pure faith. Paul reached up and touched the spot where the hole was in his chest and it didn't hurt anymore. He stood up, half expecting to fall back down, but he felt fine, and when he looked in the mirror, the hole was gone. He turned to see his back, and that wound was gone too. Paul questioned whether he was conscious. He didn't understand what was happening, but he thought of his mother, and her faith in this ring, and he started walking through his house almost chanting the words, "To all that need hope," over and over again. The ring began to glow more brightly -- Paul could feel the warmth of the ring in his hand. "To all that need hope." He said it again and again, from the top of the stairs, in each of the bedrooms and then over and over again in his parlor.

Suddenly Paul felt dizzy and he stopped dead in his tracks. He felt like he was waking from a hazy sleep as he saw Kate and the kids come slowly into focus.

In the middle of the room his family, now perfectly clear, lay huddled together on the floor with Kate's arms around the kids like she was trying to protect them from something. Paul's heart sank when he realized that they weren't moving. They looked like they had all fallen asleep, but were they sleeping, Paul wondered. Paul slowly walked to his family, thinking the worst. He took a knee next to Kate and started to reach for her face but then stopped, afraid to go any further. "What if she's . . . ," he couldn't even finish the thought. He shook his head and tried to clear it from his mind. His hand shook as his fingers touched her soft warm skin. She was warm, he thought, and his face lit up with hope. Then he reached to touch each of his children and they too were warm. His daughter suddenly yawned and rolled tighter into Kate's arms. They were all sleeping. Paul breathed a sigh of relief. From outside he heard a familiar voice calling and he thought it sounded like Tret, his stable hand. Paul tried to wake Kate and the kids but they wouldn't stir so he carried each one of them to their beds. Kate was the last and, as he set her down, he brushed the hair from her face and kissed her cheek. When he was done he went outside to see if he could find Tret. He could still hear him calling but he couldn't make out exactly where it was coming from.

Once outside, Paul saw that Charlotte was sleeping on the porch in the rocker and several of the staff were sleeping on the lawn close to the front porch and in the grass near the barn. He kept following the voice and, as he walked his property, Paul was feeling the power of the ring -- he saw all around him hope realized and lives saved. Paul then heard the voice calling from inside the barn. As soon as he stepped foot into the entrance he saw Tret, but there was something strange and eerie about him. Paul could see him, but he seemed distant, almost like he was from a dream.

"Tret, are you okay?" Paul asked, concerned.

"I will be Mr. Paul, I will be," Tret answered.

"What do you mean you 'will be'?"

"Heaven, Mr. Paul, is a beautiful place. I have seen it and it waits for me. But, before I go, you must promise me that you will get my Margaret and the others to safety."

"What do you mean to safety? And where are you going?" Paul asked. Tret wasn't making sense.

"You are all in danger," Tret said with a cold calmness. "They will be coming back for you, as soon as they get the ship back to harbor. They will come back, with twice as many men, and they do not plan on taking anyone with them this time. The ring has great power but, as you see for yourself, it can not save everyone -- the dead will remain dead and the mortally wounded unfortunately will soon follow. Mr. Paul, you have the living, for now, and the rest of us will look forward to seeing you again one day."

The reality of what Tret was saying was sinking in. "Me too, Tret, me too," was all Paul could manage in response.

Tret continued, "You have less than two days before these men will be back at your door. Use the time wisely, Mr. Paul."

"Tret, what am I supposed to tell Margaret? How do I explain this to everyone?"

"You don't. The living will soon wake and they will have very little memory of what happened last night. The grief from loss will hit hard for some, especially for my Margaret, and I know you will want to explain everything that happened, everything I've told you, but it is better unknown. You will be putting yourself and your family at great risk if more know about the ring. They will all grieve in their own ways for those of us who have left, but they will find a way to move on. You can't tell them . . . .." Tret paused suddenly then, resignedly, concluded, "Be well, Mr. Paul."

Paul raised his hand to gesture goodbye and Tret was gone.

While everyone continued to sleep, Paul put together teams of horses and hooked up every cart and carriage on the property. He went into the house and packed everything of value that he could carry or comfortably stack onto the coach. He packed a few necessities, like food and containers of fresh water -- everything else they could buy.

Paul wrote a note to his attorney, then gathered up some legal papers and put it all in a small leather folder. He would have to entrust his attorney, Francisco Merillo, with the unpleasant task of trying to clean up the mess he was about to run away from. Paul planned that, on their way out of town, he would stop at Francisco's to give him this paperwork and to sign documents that would give Francisco limited control over Paul's property and personal and business affairs in his absence. Paul would explain everything to Francisco in person and provide him with a list of instructions on how to handle things while he was gone.

Paul's main instructions, most of the content of his written note, covered the running of his orchard, in general, and his desire to get it operating again at such time in the future that the imminent danger they now faced had passed. Francisco owned his own estate and paid others to run it so Paul knew he could handle the job when the time came to resume the work here. Under the dangerous circumstances they were currently faced with, however, Paul would need operations at his place to temporarily stop. It was Paul's hope that, during this time, Francisco would agree to employ Paul's staff at Francisco's own estate under the condition that Paul would continue to pay their wages. With Paul's staff being such loyal and capable workers, he couldn't imagine that Francisco would refuse to do this. Paul planned to tell everyone here his intentions before leaving. He would explain, without going into too much detail, that it was too dangerous to stay here at the moment and that he had made arrangements with Mr. Merillo for them to work for him for a while. Now all Paul could do was keep his fingers crossed that this worked out.

The final thing Paul needed to do was to come up with a plan for his own family. This was the hardest part because Kate's and the kids' safety was what mattered most. After what seemed like hours, Paul came to a decision. It was one that he was sure would not sit well with Kate, but that Paul knew in his heart was the only way to keep them all safe. He knew that if they stayed together as a family it would be only a matter of time before they were found. Tret had told him that they will come back, and Paul knew that they would just keep coming until they got what they wanted. The only thing that would protect his family was for Paul to separate himself from them. Kate and the children would have to go and create a new life for themselves.

Thinking back on all of this had Paul in a trance-like

state. He had walked out onto the beach and was sitting in the sand. The bottle was still in his hand, as was the forgery, but he hardly remembered leaving his house. Forcing himself to return his thoughts to the present, Paul wasn't sure how Warner had found him. He wasn't sure that he cared. Paul's only way back to his family permanently was to find the man who wanted him dead. The problem for all of these years had been that Paul never knew who that man was -- he had been chasing a ghost. For all this time Paul had been led only by the note that had been left behind:

I now have what you don't.

But now that ghost has a name, and his name is Captain Darfous Warner.

After eight long years Paul's plan had finally worked. Paul knew when he left his family behind that he would never find the pirates who had come after him as Mr. Paul. To find a pirate he had to live as a pirate, and to beat a powerful one he had to become a powerful one. He also knew that he couldn't do it alone -- he needed men, courageous men who would give their lives to protect him. For the average man this plan would have been nearly impossible to pull off, but Paul's father had left him a wealthy man and he used his wealth to his advantage. He started by acquiring a ship, and then a crew, and that is how he became Captain Paul Delham.

He wasn't sure how Warner had put together that the captain of the Rising Sea was Mr. Paul of New York but he knew it wasn't his appearance. Paul had changed so much in the past eight years that he had doubts even Kate, much less the kids, would recognize him if they saw him as Captain Delham. His hair, once short and light brown, now hung in long waves past his shoulder blades. The sun had turned his hair golden and his skin brown and he looked more like a Spaniard than the Englishman that he was. He had put on a few extra pounds over the years but, at six foot four, this only made Paul look more intimidating and it worked in his favor. Paul was truly a pirate, and not just any pirate -- he was the formidable leader, the captain, of the ship the Rising Sea. His persona was imposing, strong and unbreakable; he had the ability to read a man, to look him in the eyes and know what he was thinking even before the thought crossed his mind. Paul's men respected his strengths and, at the same time, feared them as well.

Paul looked out at the ocean and wondered if discovering who Warner is and finding him could be the end of this made-up existence. He thought of the possibility that, after eight years, his family might actually be able to reunite as one and return to the life they had shared before. Paul got to his feet, leaving the bottle in the sand, and reached into his coat pocket. He pulled out an old piece of parchment and studied it. This had been the beginning of this life of deception, and he had kept it with him all this time to remind him of all that was at stake and why he kept going. In Paul's mind the person who wrote this note was the same man who sent the poisoned letter. The wording was slightly different, but the content was essentially the same. It was just too similar to be a coincidence. Paul held the two notes up side by side and read them:

I now have what you don't.

There is no return from where
you are going!
I will soon have what you don't.

Paul felt like they were two pieces to the same puzzle and, feeling as though his real life might be closer than he had dared to hope for so long, he took a deep breath and smiled.

Pirates: Chapter 24

Loyalties Revealed

"Monk what are we doing? I thought that we were going back to the ship?" Peter asked Monk as he followed him through the crowd.

"We are," Monk answered, "but we have to make one stop first."

"Where?"

"You'll see when we get there."

Peter and Monk made their way along the main street of town. It was market day and food vendors lined the streets with their small wooden carts, selling everything from fish, to carrots, to spices. Peter recognized Magis Ale House and was about to tell Monk when Monk stopped dead in his tracks, ducked behind a large palm tree next to the Barnagate Hat Company and forcibly pulled Peter with him.

"What are we hiding from, Monk?"

"Matais!"

"Matais? Why are we hiding from him? I like Matais."

"I am not sure, exactly, but Captain Paul said that we should watch him but he should not see us."

Peter was confused. He couldn't imagine why they were sent to spy on Matais. Matais was just one of the guys. He was a good sailor and he was always one of the first men to volunteer to do pretty much anything. As he thought, Peter looked around and was surprised to see Nic down the far end of the street coming out of Sal's shoe shop.

"Monk, isn't that Nic?" Peter asked, pointing in her direction.

"Yes."

Nic was weaving her way quickly through the crowded streets.

"She looks like she's in a big hurry," Peter observed. "Should we stop her?"

"No, Peter, we can't be seen. The captain wants us only to watch. Don't say a word, no matter what happens."

"What is going to happen?"

"I don't know, but that is one reason we are here, to see what happens. The captain specifically said that no matter what, we just have to stand back and watch."

"Monk, I think Matais is trying to get Nic's attention. He is waving at her."

Just as Peter finished speaking, two very large men grabbed Nic and pulled her into the alley out of their line of sight.

Peter started to scream, "Ni . . ." when Monk put his hand over Peter's mouth. He mumbled, "Monk, we have to help her," through Monk's fingers.

"No, Peter, we can't." Monk took his hand away.

"Why, Monk? Why can't we help? They are going to hurt her!" Peter said with urgency.

"Matais should be helping her, Peter."

"But he isn't! He is just standing there watching."

Just then, both Peter and Monk thought they heard Nic scream for help and yet Matais only stood there. Suddenly, they saw Matais run towards the alley, but he stopped just short of entering it. He appeared to be looking around and then, after a few minutes, he ran down the main street and vanished into the crowd.

"Monk what just happened?" Peter demanded as he shook Monk by the shoulders. "How could we just sit here and let that happen to Nic? She's our friend and she's in danger. Why would Captain Paul want us to turn and look the other way?"

"Matais," said Monk solemnly. "He needed to see where Matais's loyalties are."

"But he sacrificed Nic!" Peter was stunned.

"No, Peter, Nic volunteered. She knew what she was doing and what the risks were. Someone is trying to hurt the captain and Matais is the only new member of the crew. He signed on within the past year, while everyone else has been with Captain Paul for years. According to Stanley, the two men who tried to poison the captain by delivering the bottle talked as if they knew personal things about you, in particular, and the only people in the entire pirate world who would know anything personal about you are members of the Rising Sea's crew."

Peter listened in disbelief as Monk continued, "Captain Paul had the ship's doctor tell Matais that Captain Paul is sick and that Nic was sent to seek out an antidote for venomous sartosus, a rare and deadly form of snake venom. Now we just watched Nic get abducted, right in front of our eyes, with Matais standing watch. The captain's suspicions turned out to be true."

"Yes, it looks like Matais is playing for the wrong team," Peter agreed, "but now that the captain will know about Matais, now what? What is going to happen to Nic?"

"I would imagine that now we are going to rescue her."

"But how are we going to find her, Monk?" Peter

was clearly panicked. "She could be anywhere!"

"That is where Matais comes in, Peter. He doesn't know that we are on to him."

"He will never tell us where she is," said Peter.

"The captain has a plan, Peter, and I think it will work."

"I have asked you repeatedly what you know and what is going on, Monk, and you keep telling me, 'I don't know'," Peter said mockingly, "but yet you seem to know everything, don't you, Monk?" Peter's annoyance was evident.

"Peter, I didn't want to tell you what we were doing because I didn't want to upset you," Monk said matter of factly.

"Upset me? How? Nic was just taken right in front of us! How could you have upset me more than I already am?"

"I could tell you that Matais was promoted to Quarter Master."

"What!" screamed Peter. "That is *my* job! I was supposed to be promoted to that job."

"I told you you could be more upset."

Ignoring Monk's comment, Peter repeated, "That was my job, Monk."

"It was, Peter, but I think the word *was* means past tense. Peter, it *was* your job."

Peter glanced over at Monk and gave him a dirty look.

"Monk, don't start with the English lessons now, please. It's not funny. Why would the captain give Matais my job?"

"Because you have been demoted -- that's my first guess -- and the position then went to the next in line."

"Monk, please stop messing with me."

"Okay, Peter, what happens when the captain is not able to do his job?"

"The quarter master takes over the command of the ship until the captain can return to duty." Peter was nearly paralyzed by the thought of Matais taking command.

"Exactly. So Matais will become commander of the ship because the captain is ill, and it will become his job to rescue Nic."

"That's the plan?"

"That's it," said Monk.

"They will know we are coming," said Peter.

"Yes, that is true."

"We will be walking into a trap." Peter was a bit confounded by the transparency of this.

"Yes, but they won't know that we know it's a trap."

Peter shook his head in disbelief and said, "Monk, I have to ask, is this a plan that you came up with? I hate to be insulting but, I have to tell you, this idea sounds so dumb that only you could have thought of it."

"Well, Peter, that *was* insulting but, yes, I did have

some part in coming up with this plan."

"I am shocked, I am totally in shock. I can not believe that anyone, let alone the captain, agreed to go along with this plan. Just pinch me to make sure that I am not dreaming."

Monk reached over and pinched Peter hard on the back of his arm.

Peter yelled, "Ouch! That hurt!" Peter rubbed his arm and shot Monk another dirty look. "I didn't really mean for you to pinch me."

"Well, now you know it's not a dream," Monk said laughing.

"I can't believe you really think it's a good idea to sail our ship right into the hands of our enemies and, even more shocking, that Captain Paul agreed to this."

Monk shrugged. "He did."

"I don't understand why he would do that." Peter sounded defeated.

"Because it is the only way to find the man behind the plot to kill Captain Paul."

Peter sighed. He hated to admit it, but it kind of did make sense. "Okay, so, what about the poison?"

"What about it?" said Monk.

"Nic was supposed to find out what was used on the note and now she is gone. I think before we walk into the enemy's trap we should at least find out what Dr. Sal had to say."

"I think that is a good idea," said Monk. He smiled at Peter.

As they walked down the street to Sal's Shoes it occurred to Peter that he was now without a job. "Monk, did the captain say what my new job is going to be?"

"No, he didn't, but I did hear that Melvin needs some time off to recover from his head injury so there is definitely a spot open in the kitchen."

"In the kitchen," said Peter, visibly deflated. "I don't even know how to cook toast."

"Neither did Melvin," said Monk, and they both laughed.

Pirates:
Chapter 25

Relieved
from Duty

Matais ran though the streets, cutting through alleys, until he reached the dirt road that led to the dock. He made it back to the ship in record time -- at least it was *his* personal best. The only one on the ship who could run faster than Matais was Peter. He was hoping that he could make it back on board the Rising Sea unnoticed so he quietly sidled up the gangplank and onto the ship. But the ship's doctor was standing at the entrance with an anxious manner about him.

"Dr. Centeni, how is the captain?" Matais asked with a hint of concern in his voice, trying to cover up his annoyance at having been seen coming aboard.

"Not good, I'm afraid. Did you come across Nic?"

"No, sir, I did not," Matais lied. "I'm surprised that she is not back yet."

"I am also surprised, she knows how urgent this is. Let me know as soon as she gets back. Also, the captain is asking for Peter. Has he returned from his leave yet?"

"I have not seen him, but if I do I will send him directly to the captain's quarters."

"Thank you, Matais. You're a good man."

"You are welcome, sir."

Matais stood topside and observed as some of the crew slowly trickled in from leave while others were already preparing the ship for departure. It would be only another hour until they would set sail on their final voyage as a crew. But on this trip it would be Matais calling the shots and not Peter. Peter's demotion for insubordination put Matais first in line to be the next quarter master and things were moving along perfectly. The captain would soon have to announce his inability to command the vessel due to illness and then he will pass this duty to Matais. By morning Matais would have complete control of the Rising Sea. Of course, no crew would be left to sail the ship, but he was confident that he would find enough able-bodied seamen to set sail again within the month.

Captain Paul was holed up in his quarters with strict orders that he was not to be disturbed. He was sitting on the corner of his bed when Dr. Centeni knocked on the bedroom door.

"Doctor?" Paul confirmed.

"Yes, Captain."

"Come in quickly and shut the door." Once the doctor was in the room, Paul asked, "Doctor, did Nic make it back to the ship?"

"Not yet, Captain."

"Where is Matais?"

"He just came on board a few minutes ago."

"And what did he have to say for himself?"

"I asked him if he had seen Nic and he said he had not."

"Yes, that is what we expected him to say," the captain replied, his voice filled with disappointment. "Any sign of Peter and Monk?"

"No, not yet."

"If Peter and Monk do not make it back by the time we are to set sail we will have to delay until they get here."

"Yes, sir, I know. And what about Nic?" the doctor asked.

Captain Paul rubbed his forehead. "If she is not back yet, she is not coming back. Warner has her and when we find Warner, we will find Nic. But first, let's start to prepare . . ." A knock on the cabin door interrupted Paul and he quickly climbed into bed. "Doctor, see who it is."

"Yes, sir."

The doctor walked out of the bedroom, careful to close the door behind him, and through the outer cabin. He opened the door to find Peter and Monk looking up at him.

"Peter, come in! The captain has been waiting for you. Did you see Matais on deck?"

"No," said Peter.

"He wasn't on deck to meet you?"

"No, he wasn't there," Peter said as he stepped past the doctor into the captain's quarters. Monk followed him.

The doctor quickly scanned the part of the deck he could see and, as Peter had said, Matais was not there. The doctor closed the door behind them and led Peter and Monk to the captain's bedroom. As soon as the captain saw them he pulled the covers off and stood up.

"Do you normally sleep fully clothed, sir?" Peter said, teasing.

"Not usually, Peter, but I thought I'd be well prepared for my funeral once the poison kicks in," Captain Paul joked back.

"Okay, that is not funny," Peter responded.

"You are right, lad, it is not. It is nice to see you, though, and you too, Monk. I am glad to have you back and I want to start off by telling you both how proud I am of you. I might not be here today if it weren't for the two of you and I am grateful for that and indebted to you both. Peter, I know you and I have a few things to talk about but that conversation will have to wait until a later date. Okay?"

"Of course, Captain Paul," replied Peter.

"What I would like to know now is what you both observed in the square."

Monk spoke first. "Matais is a traitor, that is what we observed. Not only did he stand by and watch as two of Warner's men grabbed Nic and pulled her into an alley, he actually signaled to them to let them know that she was coming."

Captain Paul shook his head and clenched his jaw. "That is what I suspected," he said. "With this disappointing news we will move forward with our plan of attack."

"Captain, we need to get started," the doctor asserted.

"Yes, Doctor, you're right. It's time . . ." the captain began, but stopped when he saw that Monk was waving his arms at him to get his attention. "Monk, my friend, what is it?"

"I think Dr. Sal wanted you to have this," Monk said as he handed the captain Nic's old brown satchel.

"Thank you, Monk." Then, turning to face Dr. Centeni, Paul asked, "How long until you are ready to set sail, Doctor?"

"It will take me no more that twenty minutes, sir."

"Good. I will see you in twenty minutes, then . . . and, Doctor? Can you take this with you, please?" The captain held out Nic's bag and they all watched as the good doctor took it and slipped quietly out of the room. When the door was fully shut, he continued, "Peter, in twenty minutes I will be handing over my command to Matais. I am sure that Monk has filled you in on our plans?"

Peter nodded, and the captain carried on. " I assure you that your demotion is temporary and the quarter master's job will be yours but, for the time being, you will be filling in for Nic in the lookout. This is an important job under the circumstances, as it is obvious that Matais's plans are to lead us like sheep to the slaughter."

"Is there no other way?" Peter asked, almost pleading.

"I have exhausted myself trying to think of another plan, but Matais is our only link to Warner. He will lead us directly to him, of that I am certain. On the other hand, what Captain Warner has planned for us once we are there is a complete mystery. One thing I do know is that he won't be inviting us in for tea. We all, the crew, must be ready for a fight. However, Matais must think he is in total control right up to the point where we know we can continue without him. Do you understand,

185

Peter?"

"Yes, sir, I do."

"You -- everyone -- must take care to act perfectly normal. If Matais gets suspicious for any reason he will lead us astray faster than you can blink and we will lose any hope of getting Nic back."

"I understand," Peter assured him.

"Good. Now I want you to go out and find Matais. Tell him that you just came from my quarters and I asked you to tell him to assemble the crew because I will be on deck in five minutes to make an announcement. Monk, I want you to go to the galley and see if Stanley and the doctor need any help with the send off toast." The captain pointed his finger at the door. "Now go."

When Peter and Monk were gone, Paul put on his grandfather's white wig and dusted his face with the perfect amount of white powder to make himself look pale. After days of laying down while still fully dressed, his clothes were wrinkled and definitely smelled a bit ripe. No one would question by his appearance that he had, in fact, been poisoned.

Less than ten minutes later the doctor returned. "You look dreadful, Paul," he commented. "I think you need a physician."

Paul laughed and said, "Thanks, Doc. When you find a real one, send him to me."

Dr. Centeni smiled. "I will certainly keep an eye out

for one. Are you ready to do this?"

Paul took a deep breath. "Yes, I am."

"Okay. Now, remember, you are dying, so try to appear frail. Use me as a crutch, speak unnaturally slow and cough a few times, weakly -- it will give your performance a nice touch."

Paul smirked. "Thank you, Dr. Death, for the tips on how to die properly."

"My pleasure," the doctor replied as he pointed sharply at the door to indicate that it was time for them to go.

As Paul and the doctor slowly walked out onto the deck, the crew was waiting in silence, gathered in two perfectly straight lines. Peter and Monk were somewhere in the back row, as far away from the action as they could get, and Matais was front and center, standing at attention. Paul looked older and indeed sickly -- some of the crew even gasped when they saw him.

Paul spoke slowly, and hardly loud enough for all to hear, "Men, as you have all been made aware . . .." Paul stopped, coughed several times, and then resumed talking, ". . . someone has made an attempt on my life by poisoning me. At this time I am battling to stay alive, but the poison that was used is deadly and my fate, uncertain. Our good ship's doctor here is doing his best to try and save me."

Paul paused here and clung onto the doctor. It looked like his knees were going to go out from under him and a few men from the crew took a step forward as if they might need to catch him. Paul feebly raised his hand and they returned to attention. When he regained his balance, he continued,

"I am in no condition to command this ship at this time, as you can see, so, in a few minutes, I will be handing my command over to our new Quarter Master, Matais Andrelli. When I do, I expect you all to give him the same respect that you have given me through the years. But, first, Stanley, where are you?"

"I am right here, sir," Stanley quickly replied while running up to him.

"The mugs, Stanley."

Stanley nodded knowingly, then rushed around the deck handing out mugs of brew that he had prepared especially for this moment. When he was finished passing out the mugs, only two remained -- one that would have been Nic's, if she was here, and one intended for the quarter master, Matais.

"Matais," the captain said, raising his hand slightly to indicate that Matais should step forward.

"Yes, Captain," Matais replied as he dutifully marched over to where the captain was standing.

The captain took one of the remaining two mugs and handed it to Matais. "Drink with us, lad. I know you don't normally like the brew, but this is an important occasion for you."

Matais looked at the captain's face. He looked so sickly, a mere shadow of his former self. Matais knew that he was close to glory now and he could hear the words echoing in his head, "Captain Matais Andrelli." Now that was something worth drinking to.

"Absolutely!" said Matais, as he took the mug from the captain's hand.

"I have enjoyed sailing with each and every one of you and it is my wish to have this one last drink with my men." The captain paused to clutch his stomach, appearing to be in great pain. "I raise my glass to you. You are truly my friends and my family. Salute."

The crew raised their glasses and, almost in unison, called out, "Salute!"

Matais clinked his glass against the captain's and proceeded to drink every last drop. This was a drink that he enjoyed very much -- it had the taste of coconut, with a hint of strawberries, and, best of all, the sweet smell of victory.

Captain Paul had one last thing to say. "Matais, the ship is yours to command, lad. Make me proud."

"Yes, sir," Matais said with conviction.

The crew all watched as the captain stumbled across the deck, with the help of Dr. Centeni, back to his quarters. As the door shut behind them, most of the men said a silent prayer to themselves and made peace with the fact that it was probably the last time they would see Captain

Paul. But Matais quickly snapped them out of their reflective state as he commanded,

"Men! Give me your attention!"

The crew turned to face Matais as he stood before them in the same spot the captain had just left. Now that he had their attention, he continued, "Most of us have been friends for some time, but now I must become your commander, as well. We all have our jobs to do and, in order for me to assume my new position, I ask that you follow me the same as you did Captain Paul. Can you do that?"

A few of the men quietly replied, "Yes, sir."

"I didn't hear you," Matais said loudly. "What was your answer?"

"Yes, sir!" the entire crew responded at once.

"I am glad to hear that. Now, I'm sure that most of you have taken notice that Lookout Nic is missing from our midst today. She was sent out to find an antidote to help cure Captain Paul and she never returned. It is our belief that the same people who poisoned the captain are also responsible for her disappearance. Our mission today is to set out to find Nic and bring her home. Are you with me?"

This time the crew did not need to be prompted to respond. "Yes, sir!" they called out.

"Our mission today," Matais went on, "is also to capture the perpetrators and bring these scoundrels to justice. Are you with me?"

Again, "Yes, sir!" The crew were all hooting and cheering.

Matais smiled as he watched and listened to his newly acquired crew and couldn't help but think to himself, "I've got you all." Matais was careful to maintain a calm and concerned demeanor, but he was giddy with callous power on the inside. To the men he ordered,

"Then it's time, sailors! Man your stations and let's set sail. Stefano, hoist the anchor. Now! Let's go. Fernando, set course due west and adjust forty degrees left every twenty clicks."

"Where are we going, Matais?" Fernando asked.

"We will know when we see it." Then, up to Peter and Monk, who were manning the lookout, Matais called out, "Keep an eye out for hostiles, Peter. We need to stay well out of their sight line, if possible, and, if not, at least out of firing range."

"Will do," Peter called down, then, under his breath, mockingly, added, "Quarter Master Matais."

"Peter, remember what the captain said." Monk was looking at him disapprovingly.

Peter huffed. "Did you hear how he talked to me? Look out for hostiles -- did he really think he had to tell me that? What did he think I was going to do up here, take a nap? Or maybe he thought we were going to be checking out the native hula girls."

191

"Did you see hula girls?" Monk asked, sounding excited.

"No, I did not see hula girls." Peter rolled his eyes.

"I love hula girls," said Monk. "It is *amazing* how they can shake their hips that fast and their heads never move. They're like reverse bobblehead dolls."

"Monk! There are no hula girls!"

"I know. You don't have to yell. I am just saying that I like them."

"Fine, I get that you like them."

Not a minute passed before Monk said, "Peter?"

Peter looked over at him. "What is it now, Monk?"

"The nap sounds like a good idea, too. Do you mind if I take one?"

"Are you kidding me?"

"No. I always get tired after watching hula girls. I don't know why, since they're the ones doing all the work, but it makes me sleepy."

"Monk," Peter was trying to keep his tone from showing his annoyance, "you didn't see any hula girls."

"Well, then, I guess it doesn't matter whether I am thinking of them or actually watching them because I feel a little sleepy now."

"I don't care. Take a nap if you want," Peter said, no longer caring if Monk could hear the disgust in his voice.

Monk scooted down into the bottom of the crow's

nest and curled himself into a ball. Peter continued looking through the telescope, moving it from side to side to make sure he was seeing everything around them. Monk was fidgeting, having a hard time getting comfortable.

"Peter, I can't fall asleep," Monk complained.

"Why not?"

"I can't stop thinking about the hula girls."

"Monk, will you stop it with that already and just go to sleep."

"I will if you promise something."

"What is it?"

"If you do see hula girls, promise you'll wake me."

"I promise you, if I spot them, you'll be the first to know."

"How can I be the first to know? You'll be the first to know, won't you? And how will I know at all if I'm sleeping?"

"Ha, ha," Peter said, while thinking to himself that this must be what it's like to have a really annoying little brother. "I said I will *wake* you. Now, just go to sleep."

Satisfied with this answer, Monk was snoozing like a baby within a few seconds.

As the Rising Sea sailed along, Peter kept diligent watch but, from time to time, he would glance down at the deck and watch Matais as he barked out orders. He could see that Matais was taking his new position very seriously and, he had to admit, he was good at it. He was so good at it that Peter began to have serious doubts that this was his first time running a ship or a full crew.

Pirates: Chapter 26

The Set Up

In Captain Warner's mind, the game wouldn't be over until he made sure that the Rising Sea was at the bottom of the ocean. He disposed of the captain and now he would get rid of the last two things that Captain Paul had loved so dearly: his ship and that boy, Peter. He knew that with Captain Paul gone the Rising Sea's crew would probably disband. He had to give them good reason to come after him and Lookout Nic was it. She was important to them and they were coming for her -- he knew it in his blood. He was so caught up in these thoughts that a loud rap on his door sent Warner's heart racing.

"Who is it?" yelled Warner, his typically calm demeanor

giving way a bit to his current anxious state.

"First Mate Pantuzzo, sir."

"Enter."

Pantuzzo stepped into the captain's cabin. He was dressed in full battle attire.

"You're dressed for a fight, Mr. Pantuzzo?"

"Yes, sir."

"Does that mean that they are on their way?"

"They are indeed, Captain. I just got word that they set sail thirty minutes ago."

"And their captain?"

"Last word was that he was still alive but suffering greatly and weakening quickly."

Warner took that news with mixed feelings -- suffering and weak was good, he thought to himself, but not good enough.

"Last word?" The captain screamed so loudly the whole ship could hear him. "Last word, you say? And whose words do you hold so true that you believe this? I am starting to fear that he is in control of his own fate. That is what I believe to be true!" Warner slammed his fist on the arm of his chair in anger.

"No, sir, that is not true," said Pantuzzo, not backing down.

"Then tell me who is your source and ease my mind."

"Captain . . . " said Pantuzzo, hesitating.

"Now!" Warner demanded. "I am not asking you, Mr.

Pantuzzo. I am telling you to reveal your source."

Pantuzzo's face turned white and he dropped his gaze to the floor. He did not answer.

"If you wish to remain on my ship, Mr. Pantuzzo, you will tell me now. Now!" The captain's voice took on a steeliness that made Pantuzzo's blood run cold. He looked the captain in the eyes as he responded,

"It's your son, sir. It is Cali."

Warner's expression changed instantly to one of disbelief. He audibly gasped and, when he spoke, his words came out in a whisper. "It can't be. Cali? He has been missing for almost a year."

"It is true, sir. He signed on with Captain Delham the day he went missing."

Captain Warner was trying to understand what he was being told and his nerves were getting the best of him. He wanted someone's head on a platter right about now and Pantuzzo's looked perfect.

"Mario, how long have you known about this?" Warner asked with fire in his eyes. "He is my son! How could you let me think he was dead for all this time? You knew I thought he was dead. I have grieved for him an entire year." Warner was visibly shaking with rage. His eyes locked with Pantuzzo's. "How long have you known?"

"Sir, I swear to you, I just found out today. I have been dealing with a third party for some time now and all I knew, until today, was there was a new boy on the

Rising Sea who signed on about a year ago."

Warner was still in shock. "How didn't we find this out when we checked the ship's crew list?"

"Because he lied, sir. He took another boy's name. Matais, I believe. Sir, I saw him myself, as clear as day, today in the square. I saw him. He was the boy who signaled to our men that Meloni was coming."

"Did you confirm this with your third party?"

"Yes, sir, we did."

"Does Cali know that we plan to blow that ship out of the water, Mr. Pantuzzo? Does he know that?"

"Yes, sir, he does."

Warner's expression softened. "And still he stayed on the ship?"

"Captain, as I started to tell you, he is who I heard from about Captain Delham's condition. He sent word before departure that Peter Nichols was demoted in rank for insubordination and the next in line for the job was Cali. Right before they set sail, Captain Delham stepped down as the ship's commander due to grave illness."

"So what you are telling me is that my boy is commander of that vessel? That is what you are telling me, isn't it?"

"I'm afraid so, Captain."

"Why, Mr. Pantuzzo? Why is he bringing it here?"

"He wants the ship, sir. That is the deal we made with him. He will bring us the captain and the ring and we will capture and dispose of the crew. The ship is his. If he didn't turn out to be who he is, our plan would have been to double-cross him and sink the ship."

Warner was dumbfounded by all of this. "I would have bought him his own ship, why does he want that one? There has got to be a reason."

"If there is, sir, I don't know what it is. How do you want to proceed?"

"If you are dressed in your battle gear, Mr. Pantuzzo, I would guess that you wish to carry out the double-cross and kill my son with the rest of them?"

"No, sir. I would not presume to make decisions about this ship's course. That is your role, Captain. I figured that we would proceed with your son's plan for the time being, capture their crew, and then you can decide what to do about your son. I am dressed for battle in the event you choose a different outcome after the fact, sir. I want to be prepared for whatever comes our way."

Warner took a deep breath, his face filled with disappointment. "I didn't want to battle them, Mr. Pantuzzo. I wanted it to be a surprise. I wanted to sit out on the deck with a cold drink and listen to the boom boom of cannon fire, watching from a safe distance as we blew them to pieces a little at a time. I wanted to watch as whomever survived surrendered, and then I wanted to walk into their captain's quarters and take that ring off his lifeless finger. Now we have no choice but to draw swords," said Warner sadly.

"We will have to hold them only for ten or fifteen minutes tops. The railings along the main deck have been brushed with faltrum venom. Seconds after they touch the railings to board and invade our ship the poison will seep into their veins -- then the clock starts ticking. They will drop like flies in the middle of battle and, once that starts, they will not have a chance. Our numbers will stay large as theirs dwindle down to zero."

"My son hasn't given us much of a choice has he?"

"No, sir, he has not."

"Well then, Mr. Pantuzzo, let us prepare for battle, shall we?

"Yes sir."

As Pantuzzo turned to leave the cabin, Warner added, "By the way, where is Miss Meloni? I would love to have a word with her. I dumped her satchel out on the map table and now I have quite the mess to clean up. But, first, I do have a few questions for her."

"I will send someone to fetch her, sir."

Pantuzzo disappeared from the room and Warner walked over to the map table to begin his task of cleaning up the mess created by the contents of Lookout Nic's bag. He picked up pieces of wet glass, touching them carefully so as not to cut himself, and set them into a small wooden bucket. When he finished with the glass fragments, he picked up two pieces of parchment and unrolled them. He had already looked at them several times throughout the day but the writing had been compromised. He could see clearly that one was a note made out to Dr. Sal, but the fluid from the broken antidote bottles made the rest of the writing impossible to read. The second paper had no writing on it at all.

There was a knock on the cabin door.

"Please do come in," Warner said warmly as he opened the door and saw Nic's face. "Good evening, Miss Meloni."

Nic didn't say a word. She just stared at him as she was nudged into the room from behind.

Warner continued, "You can go, Mr. Selmo. I would like to talk to Miss Meloni -- Nic -- alone." Warner smiled and, in his best grandfatherly voice, said, "Nic is your real name, is it not?"

Still staring at him, Nic answered, "Yes."

"We are making progress. You can speak, very nice. Now, Nic, I just got some very bad news but there are a few minor details that my first mate seemed to be lacking in his report to me and I was hoping that you could fill in the holes. Do you think you can do that for me?"

"No, I am not helping you," Nic said flatly.

"I didn't really think you would," Warner said, starting to laugh, "but I am going to ask you anyway. Let's see how good of a liar you are, okay? First, let me start with these two pieces of paper that I am holding. This one is addressed to Dr. Sal but I can't read the rest. Now, I know you aren't going to tell me what it said, so I won't bother to ask, but I don't have to read past 'Dear Dr. Sal' to know that this letter was written by your captain. I have corresponded with him from time to time and, as luck would have it, I've saved a few of his letters. I compared the writing and, wouldn't you know, it's a perfect match. Anyway, I guess the struggle that I'm having at the moment, Nic, is that I am not convinced that he is really dying. So what I want to ask you for is your opinion. What do you think? Is your captain dying, Nic?"

Warner was surprised when Nic responded so quickly. "I assumed it was serious when they asked me to go to Dr. Sal's for the antidote, but I didn't talk to the captain directly. It was the ship's doctor who gave me those orders."

"I thought you weren't going to tell me anything?"

"No, I said I wasn't going to help you. There's a difference."

Warner laughed. "Okay. Next question, then. There are three bottles that weren't broken in your struggle with my men and none of them contain the antidote for the poison that I used on your captain. What is in them?"

"Perfume. Have you never smelled perfume before?"

Warner narrowed his eyes at Nic. "I don't believe

you."

"I don't really care what you believe. It is perfume. You can smell it if you want. Or, better yet, hand me any one of those bottles and I will put some on. I haven't bathed in two days. You can give me all three and I will take a perfume bath. It is perfume. Dr. Sal sells it in his shoe store."

Although Warner didn't like Nic's attitude, he decided to believe her for the time being and move on. "What about this parchment?" Warner held up the blank piece of paper. "What was on it?"

"It's blank. What makes you think it had anything on it?"

Warner was examining the paper while he listened to Nic's answer. Suddenly, his eyes grew wide, almost desperate, and he quickly moved over to his desk. From the second drawer he pulled out one single sheet of parchment. He unrolled the one he was still holding from Nic's bag, that kept curling back up, and secured it flat on the desk with two small gray rocks that he used as paper weights. He set the new parchment from his drawer down next to the other and just stared at the two. Nic stood watching him and she knew that he realized that the two pieces of parchment were a perfect match. Since Warner's paper was specially made for him (a tidbit of information that Dr. Sal was able to provide to Nic when he examined the note), the only way that would be possible is if the one from Nic's bag was the poisoned letter. "Whoops!" Nic thought to herself as a smug smile curled at the corner of her lips. She then tried to figure out how long she had been on Warner's ship and just how long it would be before this creep died from his own poisoned letter.

"Captain Warner, sir," Nic said very sweetly, "I know this is a bad time for you, but I really need to pee."

Pirates: Chapter 27

The Fight Begins

Matais had the ship circling the island at eight knots. He would pass his destination three times and would make his move just before the fourth. Warner's ship was situated in a small inlet that was nearly impossible to see from ships passing by, but it had a view of the southwest that gave them a great vantage point. Warner's lookout spotted the Rising Sea in the distance and called out to Pantuzzo,

"Ship spotted, sir."

Pantuzzo started the metronome and began to count the clicks. He counted each click until he heard the lookout call out again, "Ship spotted, sir," then he quickly wrote down the total on a piece of paper and began his count again. He did this three times and as he started his fourth count his heart began to beat nearly as loudly as the metronome -- he knew that the fourth pass was the important one and he stayed focused on every single tick.

Warner had had Nic removed from his cabin so he could be left alone with his thoughts. He took out a small vial of liquid from his top drawer and drank from it. He didn't know how much damage the poison had done to his body but he did know that this was one of his only hopes of survival. He couldn't believe he had been stupid enough to handle those notes in the first place, but the fact that he hadn't noticed the similarity to his own parchment made him irate. Warner clenched his hand into a fist and shook it violently, swearing that he wouldn't let anything take him from this world. He had gotten dressed for battle, with his pistol in the holster attached to his hip, and he was now ready for his imminent victory. Warner poured himself a large drink from the decanter on his sideboard, then walked to the cabin door and locked it. For extra protection he wedged a thick piece of wood under the doorknob and into a groove that was notched into the floor for this purpose. Then he walked back to his desk, sat down and took a long sip of his brandy. He would just sit in the safety of his quarters and enjoy the sounds of battle until he was summoned for his victory walk.

The Rising Sea was halfway into its last circle around the island and Matais knew the time had come. He had not been given any word on Captain Paul in hours but he knew that he was probably dead by now, or nearly there. Matais knew that he could remove the ring from the captain's finger with little or no resistance from the captain himself, but the ship's doctor would be a problem, and one that needed to be dealt with immediately.

"Stay on course," Matais instructed, "but slow down to three knots."

"Yes, sir," said Fernando.

Matais needed a diversion. He removed a small mallet from inside his jacket and, after a quick survey of his surroundings, Matais swung the mallet, hitting Fernando right on the side of his head. Fernando dropped like a ton of bricks and Matais quickly took the wheel to maintain their course. He kept his fingers crossed that no one had noticed and, as he looked around the ship for a minute or two, with an expression on his face like a kid in a candy store who had swiped a piece of bubble gum, he realized no one was the wiser. Knowing he was above suspicion, Matais called out to the three crew members who were nearest and they appeared almost instantly.

"Anton, help me here! Fernando needs a doctor."

"What happened to him?"

"I don't know. One second I was talking to him and the next he was lying on the deck. Can you take the wheel for a second so I can take a look at him?"

Matais got down on his knees next to Fernando and proceeded to examine him as if he were a doctor.

"Fernando, can you hear me?" Matais said.

Fernando groaned.

"He doesn't look so good," remarked Thomas, and Philep nodded his head in agreement.

Matais looked up when he spoke. "Philep, I need for you to take Fernando to his bunk right now, and Thomas, go see if the doctor has a second he can spare to look at him. Explain to the doctor that he passed out at the wheel, and let him know that he must have hit his head because he has a nasty cut that needs to be attended to. If he can't leave the captain's side then tell him that I understand and Fernando will just have to wait."

"Yes, sir," said Philep.

"Thomas and Philep, stay with him so that he sees friendly faces and is not alarmed when he wakes up. I will call for you if I need you to come back."

"Yes, sir," Thomas and Philep replied at the same time.

Philep picked up Fernando and carried him across the deck in the direction of the crew's sleeping quarters. Matais watched as Thomas knocked on the door of the captain's quarters and the doctor answered it. The doctor seemed irritated by the interruption, but it looked like he was letting Thomas tell his story. Matais could see that the doctor looked concerned but then he shut the door in Thomas's face. No, this is not the reaction that he wanted. Matais knew if this didn't work he would have to eliminate the doctor and risk being seen or heard in the process, but then he saw the door open again and the doctor stepped out. Thomas turned to Matais and nodded as he led the doctor to Fernando.

Matais took notice of everyone on the ship to make sure they were doing their jobs. Peter was his biggest concern, but Peter was taking his position very seriously -- he had not come down from the crow's nest for a second since they set sail and was fully attentive to his work.

"Anton, stay on course and I shall return," Matais said.

"Yes, sir."

Matais crossed the deck to the captain's quarters and entered, shutting the door behind him. He did a quick scan of the room and then walked to the door of the sleeping berth. Matais paused for a second, took a deep breath and pushed the door open. Immediately he saw Captain Paul lying in his bed -- his eyes were closed and he looked ghostly white. Matais pulled a knife from his belt and slowly inched toward the captain, careful not to make a sound. Matais could see that his breaths were small and shallow, and it seemed to Matais that the captain must already be knocking on the gates of Heaven.

Paul, in fact, had been watching Matais through squinted eyes and was alarmed to see that he had a knife in his hand as he approached the bed. He thought that maybe if he got up fast enough he could take Matais down before he knew what hit him. But Paul took too long deciding on a plan and then it was too late -- the boy was at his side before he could move a muscle. Matais knelt down next to the captain's bed and looked at his hand, which lay flat on top of the blanket. There it was, The Ring of Hope. It didn't look like anything special, Matais thought, but it was right in front of him and, in that instant, he decided that he wanted the ring. His father had everything a man could want, but it was *his* life on the line, *not* his father's, and this should be his treasure. Tonight Matais was going to stand up to his father for the first time in his life. He looked at Captain Paul's face, then back at the ring, and said out loud quietly, but in a voice filled with animosity,

"Father, if you want this ship so bad, come and get it, but the ring is mine."

Matais thought about buying his own ship; in fact, he would buy a fleet. As he thought about his future, he focused on taking the ring. Paul could feel Matais as he rested the hand with the knife against his ribs and started to slide the ring off his finger with the other hand. As he lay motionless, Paul repeated what Matais had said over in his mind. Then Paul thought, "Father? Could this boy really be Warner's son?"

Just then Paul felt the knife pushing up against his ribs and hoped that he hadn't underestimated Matais. As the ring slipped from Paul's finger, however, the pressure of the knife subsided and Matais stood up. Matais took a deep breath, smiled down at the captain as if to say, "It's mine now!" and then slid the prize onto his own finger. Matais was surprised by how perfectly it fit! It was clear to him that the ring was now his.

Peter was scanning the ship, looking for Matais, when he saw the door to the captain's quarters open and Matais walk out. Matais looked up and saw Peter looking in his direction. He knew instantly that he needed to get off the ship, and fast. Peter watched Matais as he started to walk across the deck.

"Matais!" Peter called out.

Matais began to walk faster.

"Matais!" Peter yelled again, even louder than the first time.

Now Matais was in a big hurry and his quick walk turned into an all out run across the ship. Peter's yelling had gotten the attention of the entire crew and they all watched, confused and stunned, as their appointed commander leaped over the ship's railing into the ocean.

"Man overboard! Man overboard!" voices called out from the quarterdeck and main deck. Any crew member who could leave his post came running to the side of the ship where Matais had launched himself into the sea. But within seconds the ship had distanced itself from the spot Matais went in and he was lost in the darkness.

Matais's head popped up out of the ocean and he saw the back of the ship as his eyes adjusted to the darkness.

He started shedding the weight of his clothes and boots -- he knew he needed to start swimming before he lost his sense of direction and ended up lost at sea. He also knew from the position of the ship that he needed to swim south to reach the island, and he would not stop until he got to shore. Matais swam with determination. He had The Ring of Hope and thoughts of the possibilities this presented stayed in his mind as he headed toward the island.

Back on the ship a voice rang out in the night like an angel's call from Heaven; a voice that left every man on board more shocked than Matais's leap into the ocean.

"Men, back to your posts! You have jobs to do."

Captain Paul was standing on the quarterdeck, watching his crew's reaction to Matais's actions. He, too, had seen Matais jump as he had come out of his cabin.

"Shouldn't we circle around to see if we can spot Matais, sir?" asked Anton.

"Matais is a traitor, Anton. He set Nic up to be captured and he just stole the gold band right off of my hand when he thought I was dying. We are done with him for now and if we are lucky the ocean will decide his fate. I am taking back the command of this ship immediately and you will continue forward until I say otherwise. Peter, tell me what you see, lad?" Captain Paul called up to the lookout.

Peter looked at the captain and realized that he had

gotten so caught up in Matais's stunt that he hadn't looked through the telescope for more than five minutes. "Sorry, Captain, I got distracted for a second. It won't happen again."

"It better not, Peter. Get back to work and let me know if you see anything. Anton, be prepared to stop this ship when I tell you to."

"Yes, Captain," Anton responded confidently, though he was truly perplexed. "How could a man so close to death all of a sudden have so much life?" he asked himself.

The crew went back to work with an attitude of excitement. They had their captain back! He didn't look like he was one hundred percent healthy, but they figured he was probably still shaking off the poison. Captain Paul hadn't planned on coming out of his cabin this soon, so his face was still white from the powder he had applied, but the commotion caused by Matais's jump overboard prompted him to emerge sooner. The captain had no idea, of course, that Matais was going to abandon ship like that. What the captain did know is that Matais didn't dive into the ocean without a plan -- Warner had to be close. Matais had slowed the boat down to a crawl and Paul wanted to know why. Paul looked up at the sky as he thought about this and saw how beautiful the night was with all of the stars. It reminded him of Starry Cove . . . and an idea crossed his mind.

"Anton," called the captain, "what is our course?"

"We have be circling the island, Captain."

"We have be circling the island all night?"

"Yes, sir. For a few hours now, sir."

"Anton, take it down to two knots, now."

"Aye, aye, Captain."

"Does anyone know how many times we've circled this bloody island?"

"Almost four, sir," said Fernando as he walked out onto the deck accompanied by Thomas and Philep. "I heard you back at the helm, Captain, and I figure that if you can command a ship while you're dying, I can do my job with a little bump on my head." Fernando was smiling as he approached the ship's wheel.

The captain smiled back. "Are you sure, Fernando?"

"Yes, I'll be fine. It's good to have you back, sir," he said as he took the ship's wheel.

"Thank you, Fernando. How far do you think we are into the fourth lap?"

"Let's see, he knocked me upside the head at about three and a half and we were doing eight knots at the time . . ."

"But he had me drop it down to three knots just minutes after they carried you off," Anton interrupted, "so we can't be more than three quarters into the fourth."

As he listened, Paul kept thinking about Starry Cove. Specifically, he thought that if this island has places like Starry Cove, Warner probably has his ship docked somewhere that keeps it hidden from passing ships. Matais obviously slowed the ship down to three knots to give himself time to get the ring and get off of the ship.

"Fernando, if Captain Warner is planing a surprise attack the only way he could surprise us is if he knows exactly where we will be and when, right?"

"Yes, sir."

"So we've circled the island at the exact same speed three full times but on the fourth time around Matais had Anton slow it down by five knots."

"Do you think they are timing us, Captain?"

"Yes, I do, and Matais jumping ship tells us they have to be very close by."

"What do you want to do, Captain?" asked Fernando.

"Fernando, make a hard left and take us towards the beach."

"Aye, aye, Captain."

"Peter, watch for the island and keep us one hundred yards from the shoreline so we don't run aground," Captain Paul called out.

"Aye, aye," Peter answered.

"Anton, be prepared to drop anchor."

"Yes, Captain."

The Rising Sea came to rest quietly and Paul had half the crew prepare themselves to go to shore. The small exploration boats were lowered into the water with five men in each. Monk went straight to the beach with Thomas and Philep while the rest of the crew positioned themselves along the shoreline in their boats. Peter was in the lead boat with the telescope, following Monk's movements on the beach. Monk had climbed to the top of a palm tree at a bend in the coastline and, with a little help from the moon, he saw Warner's ship nestled in an inlet, facing out and ready to set sail. The ship was twice the size of the Rising Sea and the inlet didn't look big enough for that ship, or any ship for that matter, to turn around in. Monk wondered how they had gotten themselves in there like that. The only explanation he could come up with was that the inlet led to a much larger area. After more than an hour, Peter was excited when he finally saw Monk's signal. He, in turn, signaled the others and all the boats headed to the beach.

By Mario Pantuzzo's calculations, Matais should be leading the crew from the Rising Sea down the shoreline by boat. In ten more minutes, Pantuzzo would take the ship out six hundred yards, into their line of sight. But no sooner had he thought this than he heard the lookout call out, "Ship spotted, sir." Pantuzzo thought he must have heard wrong. Matais said they would pass three full times and set anchor before the fourth -- why are they passing again? He couldn't even give chase from their current location. Then he thought about the ring. It was more than possible that Matais wasn't able to get the ring off of the captain yet and had to circle another time. Unable to

216

confirm anything at this point, all Pantuzzo could do is start counting again.

Paul and his crew navigated through the jungle and positioned themselves just inside the tree line, where they couldn't be spotted from Warner's ship. Monk climbed to the top of the tallest palm tree he could find and, with the telescope, scanned the ship. He counted all the men on deck and figured there were more below deck that weren't visible. Monk came down and returned to the captain. Captain Paul and the crew were huddled together, waiting for Monk's report.

"Monk, what did you see?" Paul asked.

"I counted twenty-two men on deck. I also saw three ladders down and two boats missing off the starboard side. I scanned the inlet and I could see both boats -- two men in each, sitting about three hundred yards southwest, with telescopes. I think they are waiting for us to come up the coastline."

"Good," said the Captain, "we outnumber them top-side. If we can take out most of the men on deck we will be evenly matched to take on the rest of their crew. We have the element of surprise on *our* side now and we need to make it pay off. We will go up the ladders on the starboard side and shimmy down the rail until everyone is in place. I want you to stay in pairs and watch each other's backs. I don't want to lose anybody. Monk, you are going to be my eyes on that ship. I need you to go back up that

217

tree and make sure we have the clearest path on board. We don't want to give ourselves away going over the rail. Give me one long wave if the coast is clear and two short ones if we need to wait." Paul demonstrated both. "Got it?"

"Aye, aye, Captain," Monk said, feeling like a real pirate.

"When I get Monk's signal that it is safe to go, I will give you all the dead man's fist and we'll head out. Remember to work together and watch your partners' backs."

Paul started into the inlet first. He expected that he would be able to touch bottom initially, before the water became deep, but instead found himself immediately underwater. Peter watched as Paul's head surfaced and then Peter and the rest of the crew followed suit. It took a few seconds for their bodies to adjust to the coolness of the water. Once Paul could see that they were all in, he started to swim towards the ship, trying not to make any noise. It was no more than one hundred feet from the inlet bank to the ship -- an easy swim, and it didn't take long for them to get into place.

Captain Paul and Peter got to the ship first and they began to climb silently up the ladders. As they approached the top, they each grabbed hold of the rail and slid down the side, trying to get into place. Paul could hear footsteps and men talking and then, from where he was, he could see Monk doing a double wave. Paul stopped moving and kept his hands motionless on the rail. Turning his head slightly, he saw Peter was doing the same. Everyone was watching the captain, ready to go; they just needed the right moment. Monk could see through the telescope that Paul was waiting on him so he quickly refocused the scope from spot to spot, making sure he saw every part of the ship. The two men nearest the captain and Peter were just making rounds, stopping for a second every dozen yards or so to look around and listen, and then moved on. Monk saw them walking away from Paul and, as the distance grew between them, Monk knew it was time. Paul saw Monk's single long wave and Paul gave the crew the dead man's fist.

"Peter, you stay near me no matter what happens, do you understand?" Captain Paul whispered.

"Yes, sir, I've got your back," Peter whispered in reply.

"And I yours, lad," Paul said as he climbed over the railing.

Once on deck, Paul could see the two men they had heard talking. He and Peter gingerly crossed the deck until they stood almost on top of them. Paul then gave Peter a nod and each pulled out his pistol. When they were within range, they simultaneously swung the butt ends of their pistols at the back of the sailors' skulls. As they made contact, the two men, like puppets with their strings cut from above, collapsed on top of one another. Paul nodded to Peter again, signaling for him to follow him. Paul could see the doorway to Captain Warner's quarters, but to get there they had to cross the ship, go up eight steps, cross a small deck area . . . and get past one very large, very muscular pirate who was standing guard.

Paul grabbed Peter and together they ducked against one of the masts so they were out of sight of the guard. Speaking quietly, Paul said,

"Peter, we need to take down that guard now, before anyone knows we are on this ship. Unfortunately, there is no way to get up to where he is stationed without being seen, so I'm going to need your help. If I am the one he sees, he is going to shoot me on the spot, no questions asked. If he sees you, on the other hand, he won't react the same way. You're much smaller, and young, so he won't feel intimidated."

"So, what are you saying?" Peter asked. He was pretty sure he knew, but he was hoping he was wrong.

"I need you walk over to the steps and go up them."

"Up the stairs," Peter said nervously. "Those stairs over there, by the giant pirate dude."

"Yes, up those stairs."

"Um . . . he's not going to like that."

"No, he's not, and that is what I am counting on. I need for you to distract him."

"Captain, he could shoot me. Small and young or not,

he might just shoot." Peter was having a hard time not raising his voice above a whisper.

"He won't just start shooting," Paul reassured him, hoping that it was true. "Peter, just talk to him. Tell him you're the captain's son and you want to see him. That should buy me enough time to work my way up behind him."

"His son!" said Peter. "What if he doesn't *have* a son?"

"Don't worry, Peter, he has a son. Actually, it was . . . it *is* Matais. We don't have time to get into this right now, but it's true. Just try to keep a little distance between you and him in case he knows what Matais looks like. Right now it's dark enough that if he doesn't get a good look at you he won't be able to tell that you're not him."

"Matais is his son? But his last name isn't Warner." Peter's mind was stuck on this whole Warner's-son-being-Matais bombshell.

"No, it's not. He lied about who he is. I think it's safe to assume that Matais is not his real first name, either, so don't call yourself that. Just say you're his son. We have to move on this now, but Peter? Be careful," Paul said, sounding concerned.

"Be careful? Oh, yeah, that's what I'll do, I'll just be careful," Peter said sarcastically as he began walking towards the steps and the hulking pirate from the land of giants. "I'm sure a bullet or two won't hurt too much, or maybe he will just squash my head with his bare hands." Peter shot one more glaring look at Paul and then focused on getting to the stairs.

Paul stayed in the shadows as he watched Peter approach the steps. As soon as Peter was within three feet of them, Paul saw the guard look in Peter's direction. No sooner did Peter's foot touch the first step than the guard's rifle was drawn and pointed right at him.

"Stop right there or I will shoot," the guard growled. "State your business, intruder."

Peter was scared and at a complete loss for words. Paul was more than a little concerned, and still too far away from them to help.

"I said *state your business*. Speak up now or I am going to shoot you where you stand."

"I wouldn't shoot me if I were you," Peter said, sounding much more confident than he felt.

"You're not me, boy." The guard repositioned his rifle at Peter.

"Put one bullet in me and my father will feed you to the sharks."

"Your father?" The guard lowered his gun ever so slightly. "What are you talking about?"

"Your dear captain, Darfous Warner, is my father, and I can assure you that if you shoot me, your life will be worthless." Peter's voice grew stronger as he spoke since he realized that the jumbo pirate hadn't shot him yet.

Pantuzzo, still keeping count of time to try to determine the Rising Sea's position, was on click three thousand, one hundred and fifty-two when heard someone say, "is my father." "Cali?" he thought, then turned to see gunner mate Stiller talking to a boy standing on the steps. It was too dark for him to see the boy clearly, but who else could it be.

"Cali," Pantuzzo called out. "What are you doing here?"

This startled Peter and he took one step backwards, preparing himself to flee if necessary. Stiller recognized Pantuzzo's voice, however, and visibly relaxed a little when he heard him address Peter in a familiar manner. He kept his eyes on Peter, waiting to hear if Pantuzzo would continue speaking, but before Pantuzzo could say another word his world went black and Philep eased his body to the deck. Philep stood up quickly and remained perfectly still, afraid to move, as he saw the lookout gazing down at the deck. He was relieved when the lookout focused his attention elsewhere, and by the time Stiller finally looked in Philep's direction, he was just a figure in the night with, Stiller thought, a familiar voice.

"What is going on out here?" Warner screamed as he poked his head out from his cabin. "Mr. Stiller, why are you not directly at my door?"

Stiller started thinking of the horrible things that the captain might do to him if he was told that Stiller was just

223

about to shoot his son, and said quickly, "I was talking to your son, sir."

Matais's dive into the ocean was looking really good to Peter right about now.

Paul had just pulled himself to the top of the captain's deck rail and was seconds away from taking Mr. Stiller out of the picture when Warner stepped out onto the deck. Paul froze. Peter was in serious trouble now, and he knew he could get one clear shot off at Warner from where he was, but then he would have to go at Stiller by hand and Stiller still had his rifle cocked and ready to shoot. Paul realized, however, that there were no other options. Hoping that Peter could escape before Stiller could fire, Paul raised his gun and prepared to pull back the trigger.

"My son, you say?" Warner's voice was filled with anger. "Mr. Stiller, show my son into my quarters. Cali," he yelled, "get in here now!"

To Paul's horror, Warner turned and stepped back into his cabin. Paul, keeping his eyes on Peter, quickly made his way over the top of the railing. Peter, seeing no other options, felt compelled to move forward up the steps. With each step he took, Peter felt his heart racing and he was ashamed -- he was a pirate and he should be fearless, but his hands were shaking, his knees were shaking; he was a pirate who was scared. He felt like a failure.

"Come on, boy, hurry up," Stiller urged. Stiller was waiting at the top of the stairs to usher Peter into Warner's quarters.

Peter saw Paul as he came over the top of the rail and was watching him move toward the cabin door. Peter stopped at the very last step and looked up at the sky.

"Lad, what are you doing?" Stiller asked. "Your father is waiting."

"I just noticed what a beautiful night it is, sir."

"Listen, lad, stop with this foolishness and let's go." Stiller knew that Warner did not like to be kept waiting.

"Mr. Stiller?" Peter continued stalling for time.

"What is it, boy?" said Stiller, losing his patience.

"Do you like stars?"

"Mr. Stiller!" a voice called out from the cabin. "Get my son in here *now*."

"That's it, come along," Stiller said to Peter sternly. "You heard what your daddy said. Now *move*!"

Peter didn't budge. "Mr. Stiller, you didn't answer me. Do you like stars?"

Stiller looked at Peter and clenched his teeth. Peter could see his jaw tightening and his right eye twitched.

"You're coming with me, boy," Stiller said as he bent down slightly and grabbed Peter by the arm to help him along.

Paul got to the cabin door and could not go past it without giving himself away so he took two steps back, raised his pistol at the back of Stiller's head and cocked the gun. The click of the gun got Stiller's attention and he briefly turned his head, looking back in the direction of the door. There he saw Captain Paul pointing the pistol directly at him. Stiller looked stunned, his eyes wide and questioning, and he was probably relieved when Peter's pistol came crashing sharply into the side of his face, breaking his jaw and knocking him unconscious for hours. Peter stepped over his crumpled body and onto the deck. He smiled at Captain Paul who in turn gave him a nod and then disappeared through the doorway of the cabin. Peter decided to stay outside and make sure the two captains were not interrupted.

Paul was an imposing figure -- a towering six foot four, with bulging muscles as hard as stone. The sight of Paul with a pistol in his hand and fire in his eyes should have had Captain Warner shaking in his boots. Instead, Warner was calmly sitting in his desk chair and sipping his brandy, almost unfazed by Paul's presence entirely.

Pirates: Chapter 28

Two Worlds Collide

Paul's eyes were locked on Warner expecting some defensive move but none followed. Captain Warner took a sip of his drink before speaking.

"You got me," he said, very matter-of-fact. "I truly have to hand it to you, Captain -- you got me. I was expecting to sit here in my cabin tonight with my glass of brandy and listen to your men die. The upper hand was to be ours, but it wasn't meant to be. You and your men did a magnificent job of disabling my crew and without a whimper. I am impressed, although, I must say, a bit disappointed as well. The first thing I am going to do in the morning is fire the lot of them."

"I don't think you are going to have to worry about

the morning, Warner," Paul interjected.

"At the moment that is how it looks, but appearances can be deceiving, Captain. I wouldn't get too comfortable if I were you." Warner's calm demeanor did not waiver.

Paul wasn't sure what Warner meant by this and he didn't care; he was the one holding the pistol.

Warner continued, "Speaking of looks, Paul, you look pretty good for a dead man."

"Thanks for noticing. I'm feeling pretty good, really -- the swim from shore was all that I needed to wash away what was ailing me," Paul said, knowing the ocean water had removed all the white powder from his face.

"I will have to remember to take up swimming," Warner said with a smile.

Then there was silence as Paul tried to figure out who Warner was and where he might have come in contact with him. Warner knew that Paul was trying to size him up, trying to connect the dots, and it amused him. It was all part of his plan.

Breaking the silence, Warner said mockingly, "Have you put it together yet, Captain Paul? I can see you're trying hard to figure it out but you just can't do it, can you? If you need some help, let me know. I would be happy to provide a clue." Warner's smile was smug.

"You want to play with me, Warner? Is that your game?" Paul said calmly, inching closer to him, his finger visibly tensing, putting pressure on the trigger.

Warner remained completely composed and it was obvious to Paul that he was not the least bit afraid. He seemed resigned to his fate, but that didn't weaken Paul's resolve to finish this.

"Okay, Warner, I'll admit that I don't recognize you. Your voice sounds familiar, but I can't place the face."

"I am not at all surprised. As I appear to you right now, I am a complete stranger, but I assure you that I'm not." Warner's words were edgy and cold.

Paul could hear the contempt in Warner's voice and couldn't imagine what he had done to this man. Paul just kept staring at him, trying to uncover a memory that would answer this question. His mind was racing back in time when he recollected something -- those dead eyes staring back at him in the dark. Warner saw the look on Paul's face suddenly change, his expression growing angry and his jaw clenching tighter.

"You were the one who was there. You personally tried to steal my family," Paul said, his own tone now filled with contempt. "The one thing I remember from that night is your dead gaze, and as sure as I am standing here, it was you, you who fired the gun. You didn't just send your lackeys to do the dirty work, you tried to kill me yourself."

"Yea," Warner cheered, "I'm so happy to see you remembered me! I would have been disappointed if I hadn't made an impression. So what now? You shoot me because I shot you? Honestly, Paul, I was happy to do it, and it looked like it hurt when that bullet sunk into your body. It did, right?" Warner's grin was downright sinister. "When my man pulled the ring off of your finger you didn't have a breath in your body, so I was a little surprised to find out later that the bullet didn't do its job."

"I'm sure you were," said Paul sarcastically, "and disappointed too, no doubt. But what I would have loved to have seen was the expression on your face when you discovered that my family had gotten away. I bet that just made your day, didn't it?"

"You have no idea . . ."

Paul cut Warner off and kept talking, "And what about those two fools who tried to poison me? Your doing, right? The note in the bottle came from you, didn't it? You really should think about asking for your money back for that job." Paul could see that Warner's calm exterior was starting to show cracks, and continued, "With all you have put me through, I am still standing. My family is still alive. If I were keeping score here, I would have to say that I'm winning." Paul concluded with as much smugness as he could muster, and he could see Warner was about to crumble.

Warner stood up quickly. His movement was so sudden that Paul almost shot him on the spot out of reflex. He slammed his drink down on the desk, brandy spilling and splattering everywhere.

"You're winning?" Warner screamed. He was no longer cool and collected, but, rather, seething and frenzied, as Captain Paul had clearly sliced into a nerve. Warner had tried hard to keep it bottled inside. He had wanted to stay dispassionate in his encounter with Paul, but his anger came gushing out. To make matters worse, he was unnerved that Paul was witness to his momentary loss of composure.

Paul was startled, but more so by the memories Warner's outburst brought up than by the outburst itself. He couldn't help but think that the last time he saw that much animosity erupt from a human being was the day his brother had slammed the ring on their father's desk and stormed from the room.

"No," Paul said quietly, then thought to himself, "It can't be." Charles was older than he, but by only a year, and the man standing before him was much older, at least twenty-five years his senior, if not more. Yet, it was clear.

"Charles, it's you!" Paul said in disbelief. "I should have put it together years ago. It all makes perfect sense. 'I now have what you don't'?" And Paul finally realized what this man wanted. "*My life!*" Paul yelled at his brother. "That is what you are after! That is what you have always wanted! All the years of hostility was nothing more than pettiness and jealousy. And what did you think, that without me in the picture my family would somehow be yours? You have grown old, Charles, and I may not have recognized your face, but I do know what I just saw and it is you. How could you? What did I ever do to you?"

Charles did not hesitate before responding, "What did you do? Are you kidding? You, my brother, have stolen everything from me, and don't try to deny it. You, the special one! You stole our father's love and then you pitted Mother against me. I was never given the same opportunities as you and then you came along and, with Mother's help, stole what should have been mine and mine alone. That was *my* ring!"

"This is all about that stupid ring," Paul said in disgust. "I told Mother to give it to you but ultimately it was her decision to make. I never felt good about what she did, it wasn't supposed to be mine. But I tried to make things right."

"And how, exactly, did you go about that?"

"I tried, Charles. I tried and I tried. Ask yourself how many times I came to your door asking to see you. How many, Charles?"

Charles rolled his eyes. "I don't remember."

"Well, I do -- almost every day for three straight months and then once a week for the entire next year. You had me turned away at the door time and time again, and yet I continued to try. Father's ring belonged to you, I knew that, and I was trying to give it to you. But you just wouldn't let me."

"You were trying to give it to me," Charles started to laugh. "It wasn't yours to give, Paul! I didn't want you to hand it to me like it was some second-rate prize. All of my life I have come in second to you. I was born first and yet, at every turn since you arrived, I was always an afterthought.

"Father and Mother never felt like that, I assure you."

"You don't know what they felt. Father would pull you out of the fields to teach you how to fence and leave me to tend to the hands. He'd play chess with you for hours and he took you to his favorite fishing holes. It was always about you, and then Kate came along."

Paul went on the defensive immediately at the mention of his wife. "Kate? What does Kate have to do with any of this?"

"The day she came to the house for the first time, I answered the door. She was with her grandmother and I looked at her standing there -- she was, what? Seventeen at the time? -- and she was the most gorgeous creature on earth." Charles's face softened for a moment as he relived the moment. "I had never seen green eyes before and they were so beautiful, you could get lost in them. Then she smiled at me. I must have talked to her for almost thirty minutes. It was going so well and I was excited. I had met the girl of my dreams."

"You're talking about my Kate?" Paul said, looking both surprised and confused.

"She wasn't yours, she was *mine*. Just one of the many things that you've taken from me."

"How did I take her from you, Charles? You didn't even know her."

"I was getting to know her, and then you came bursting through the front door with Father. The two of you laughing and Father patting you on the back because you had finally beaten him with the sword. You were sweaty and disgusting and she couldn't take her eyes off of you! It was like I didn't exist after that. I continued to talk but she didn't hear a word I was saying, she just watched you. But she was mine, you had children with her that should have been mine and that ring was mine!"

"So you thought that you could just take them all away from me?"

"I came so close, didn't I? I took them out of your house and brought them here to this beautiful ship. I remember how happy I was when I heard the anchor being hoisted, knowing that Kate was on board. We were setting sail for Spain. It is such a beautiful country, and I knew Kate and the kids were going to love it there."

Paul just looked at his brother. He couldn't believe what he was hearing. Charles, who was so lost in the moment that it was as if no one else was in the room,

continued talking,

"I had purchased a house on the coast some years earlier, with her in mind. I even had it decorated especially for her. I had servants waiting for our arrival so that she would be treated like a queen. I had it all in my hands and then . . . it just slipped away." Charles's face fell with disappointment. "It slipped away," he said again, softly, while looking at his right hand. "They stood right where you are now, Paul. Kate was huddled over the kids protecting them, like I was going to hurt them. I would never have hurt them. I just wanted to love them. Kate begged me to let them go, but I couldn't. I mean, you were dead, they would need someone to take care of them, right?"

Paul did not know what to say to his brother. There was nothing *to* say, so he just continued to listen.

"I tried to make her see that she needed me, now more than ever, but she just cried for you and looked at me with hatred. I even pulled your ring out of my pocket to prove to her that you were gone. I slid it onto my finger and I remember how angry she got when I did that. She screamed and called me the most hateful things. But as the ring settled into place on my finger, the strangest thing happened -- the air in the cabin turned white and hazy, like we were standing in the middle of a cloud, and as quickly as the room had changed, it changed back. It felt as though we had gone someplace, on an instantaneous trip, and when we got back, or the haze settled -- whatever it was -- Kate and the children, they were exactly the same, but I . . .," Charles paused for a second, shutting his eyes, before continuing, "I was different. I became this," he threw his arms out to display himself. "I came back in this body, old and used. Why, Paul? Why me? You wore the ring, why not you?"

Paul struggled to find the words to answer. "Charles, I don't . . ."

But Charles wasn't listening. "When I looked into Kate's eyes I saw the reflection of the man that I had become and the ring was gone. A few minutes later the room turned white again, but this time, when the haze cleared, they were gone. It was like they had never even been here, and yet I remained old. The girl that I fell in love with was gone. You had stolen her, you turned her against me, and I could see that she would never be mine. I went back to your estate looking for her, but all of you were gone. Yes, I shot you and left you for dead, but even in death, Paul, you managed to steal something from me."

"Charles, I didn't have anything to do with what happened to you. It was the ring."

"Of course it was the ring," Charles said, his anger returning. "Don't you think the first thing I thought about when Kate vanished was Father's campfire stories about the great Ring of Hope? He knew the stories so well because he had the ring, but he didn't even trust us enough to tell us."

"He was obviously trying to protect us, Charles. People would have come looking for the ring otherwise."

"You knew though, didn't you, Paul? And that is why Mother wanted you to have the ring, because she knew too."

"She didn't know for certain, Father never told her. The only thing she had to go by were the stories she had heard and the inscription on the ring. And despite my own suspicions that it was The Ring of Hope, I didn't really *know* until the day I watched Kate and the kids appear before me in that same white haze."

"Kate never told you about me, did she?"

"She didn't remember any of it. All she remembered was having dinner and then going to bed."

"And the children? What did they remember?"

"Nothing. They woke up like it was just another day. But it wasn't, of course. The ring brought them back to me, but at what cost, Charles? My days would never be ordinary again, and I have you to thank for that."

"Ah, well, Paul, a little disappointment in life won't kill you now, will it? Guess it just came as a bit of a shock to you after all those years of getting and having everything you wanted. So, where is the ring now, Paul? It's not on your hand, I see. Where is it?"

"Your son has it."

"What are you talking about?"

"Your son, Charles. He took it from me earlier this evening. He said that if you wanted the Rising Sea you could have it but the ring was his. You should be proud -- your son is a chip off the old block. He came at me, knife in hand, and took the ring right off my finger. Then he bravely jumped into the ocean with the ring he had stolen."

Charles's jaw nearly dropped to the floor and Paul could see that he was truly surprised to hear this.

"What's wrong, Charles? Was this not part of the plan? Has the prodigal son run off with the prize, or I should say in his case, *swum* off with it? I hope he is a good swimmer, Charles, because it was a long way to shore in the dark."

Charles's legs buckled under and he stumbled back into his chair. He had given the boy everything that he had ever wanted and yet he knowingly took from him the only thing left that mattered. Charles decided right then that no matter what the outcome of this night turned out to be, his son was dead to him. As he sat there, slumped in his chair, Charles looked beaten. The dark circles under his eyes suddenly seemed like they were becoming increasingly more pronounced and he was significantly paler than he had been when Paul had gotten there. He was sweating and feeling slightly nauseous, but no matter how bad he felt, he still had one satisfying thought left to brighten his day.

"At least my son is alive," Charles blurted out.

Paul looked at Charles. Calmly, he said, "You don't know what you're talking about, Charles. You have no way of knowing whether my son is alive or dead, of that I am sure."

Peter had been standing outside the cabin door this entire time, making sure that no one attempted to interrupt this meeting. He had heard most of what was being said, but this part grabbed his attention.

"Oh, but I do," said Charles. "In anticipation of our battle with your men, we decided to brush the railings of the ship with a poison similar to the one I used on the letter, but this one has a little more kick to it. Once it makes contact with the skin the victim typically has no more than fifteen minutes to live. I would bet anything that you probably brought your son along to teach him the family business, isn't that right? I even heard him outside my door here talking to Stiller." Warner, trying to smile, grimaced as he spoke.

"You seem to think you know more than you do, Charles. Tell me, who do you think my son is?"

"I have had people watching you for some time, dear Brother, and you seem very fond, not to mention protective, of that boy Peter."

"I am very fond of Peter, Charles, but you're wrong.

He is not my son, though he would make a fine one. Peter is my quarter master, a young man who I respect very much," Paul said.

Peter, taking in every word since he heard his name mentioned, was feeling pretty special. Paul's words meant a lot to him, and the fact that he got promoted to Quarter Master, finally, had him feeling quite important. He kept listening intently.

"I don't believe you, Paul," Charles said unwaveringly. "It may have been years since I saw him, that one night when he was here with Kate, but he looks too much like Mother."

Paul knew his brother well enough to know that an argument over what Charles believed to be true could go on forever. "Peter, come in here please," Paul requested.

When Peter stepped into the room Charles's heart dropped. Paul's willingness to put the boy on display so quickly made him think that maybe he was wrong about Peter's identity.

"How do you feel, Peter?" Paul asked.

"I feel fine, sir."

"Good to hear, lad. How is Mr. Stiller doing?" asked Paul with amusement.

"Sleeping like a baby, sir." Peter smiled and looked at Charles.

"Mr. Warner here was telling me of a sickness that is going around. What was it again, Charles? An allergic reaction to faltrum venom?" Paul said pointedly, revealing his secret.

Charles was now sweating profusely and gripping his stomach, but the poison that was destroying his body was nothing compared to what he heard next.

"Peter, what did the doctor tell you this morning about faltrum venom?"

"Dr. Sal said that it was very dangerous and anyone coming in contact with it would get very sick and likely die."

"So what did he suggest you do?" Paul was enjoying dragging out his conversation with Peter for Charles's benefit.

"Get vaccinated with the antidote, sir. He suggested that everyone on the ship should take the antidote, just in case."

Both Paul and Peter looked at Charles before Paul continued, "I thought that was a fantastic idea, Charles. You can never be too safe. So what did I have everyone do before we left port tonight, Peter?"

"We all took the antidote, sir."

"So Captain Warner shouldn't worry about you after all, should he?"

"No, sir, not at all."

"Thank you, Peter. You can return to your post now. Thank you for joining us and sharing that important information with Captain Warner. And Peter, could you shut the door behind you on your way out, please?"

"Aye, aye, Captain," Peter answered, still thinking about his new title.

Once Peter had closed the door, Paul spoke. "See, Charles, Peter is a fine boy. I said he would make any father proud, and he does, indeed, make his father proud. And since he was smart enough to take the antidote for the venom and, as it turns out, protect himself from your poisoned rails, you don't have anything to worry about -- he is going to grow up to be a great man, just like his Grandpa Ardin."

Charles spoke immediately, showing no reaction at all to what Paul had just said. "I knew he was your son."

Paul smiled in response. "So he is, Charles. So he is."

As Paul stared at his brother from the other side of the desk he noticed the letter he sent to Dr. Sal asking about poison antidotes. He didn't know why the only words left on the letter were "Dear Dr. Sal", but he was positive it was his writing.

Paul had known Sal for years and they were very good friends so it was lucky for everyone that Charles had sent Pantuzzo to Sal to inquire about poisons and their reaction times. Pantuzzo had told Sal that they had a rodent problem on board their ship and Captain Warner wanted something that would kill them quickly. Sal was a savvy man, having been a pirate for most of his life, so he was a little wary about Pantuzzo's rat story. His suspicions grew when Marcus and Antonio came into his office poisoned by the same venom he had recommended to Pantuzzo as the slowest acting, then Sal's worries were confirmed when Nic showed up at his door with the note from Captain Paul.

Charles looked up at Paul. Although his vision was becoming blurry, he could still see enough to know that Paul was staring at the letter on his desk.

"I took that letter off of Miss Meloni," Charles said, coughing.

"And where is Nic, Charles?"

"She is safe, Paul. I am sure your men have found her by now."

"What happened to the rest of this letter?"

"The letters got wet in Miss Meloni's satchel and the ink must have dissolved."

Charles watched with anticipation as Paul started to reach for the parchment. Charles's biggest fear was that Paul would slip through his hands -- that he would get to go back to his life with Kate and his kids and continue living his life of privilege as if nothing had ever changed. As Paul's fingertips got within inches of the poisoned letters, Charles could almost taste his victory.

Peter was still standing outside the cabin door when he heard Nic screaming from the other side of the ship. Then he saw her. She was running in his direction, but

Peter couldn't quite make out what she was saying. Whatever it was, she looked scared.

"Tell the captain what?" Peter asked when he finally understood a few words.

As Nic continued towards him, her words rang in his ears and he became aware of the urgency.

"Peter! Tell the captain that Warner put poison on all the letters! He can not touch them! Warner poisoned the letters with something different. Quick, Peter! There is no antidote for what he used!"

Peter burst through the cabin door, but he was too late. He just looked at the captain in anguish. Nic skidded to a stop in the doorway only seconds later and was horrified to see Captain Paul standing there holding both pieces of parchment. Charles sat in his chair smiling as he watched them all trying to figure out what to do next. His voice was weak when he spoke,

"As I told Miss Meloni earlier, Paul, you always have to have a back up plan. I didn't know what mouse I would catch in this trap, or if I would even live to see it work, but I am thrilled to know that after all we've been through it is you, Paul, who will be joining me."

They all turned to look at Charles. He was still smiling, his mouth partly open because he wanted so badly to laugh but just couldn't muster up the strength. He still had more to say, however, so he took a deep breath and continued.

"Peter, it was certainly nice to meet you, and your father is right -- you seem like a fine boy. I wish for your sake that he could be around to see you turn into a great man, but I'd be lying if I didn't admit that for my sake, I'm happy he won't. And Paul, it has been great catching up with you after so long . . .." Charles paused as a wave of pain ran through his stomach. When it subsided, he said, "I hate to be the party pooper but I am so tired. I can't seem to keep my eyes open. See you soon, Paul."

Charles closed his eyes and drifted into a sleep that he would never wake from. Peter turned and looked at Paul, confused and scared.

The room was silent for what felt like forever. Nic was crying and Peter just stood there in shock. Paul didn't want Peter to find out that he was his father this way, but he knew that Peter had probably heard at least some of his conversation with Charles. He also knew that everything would become clear to Peter once he had time to sit down with him and explain it. Peter had been going from one world to another for some time with the help of his magic pirate boots, so it should not come as too big of a surprise to him that Paul's ring had the power to change the way Peter saw his father in the pirate world. It was for their protection.

Then Paul thought about the ring. The Ring of Hope had protected Paul through the years in so many ways. He thought back to the day in the bathroom when his wounds had vanished and Kate and the children had been brought back. As he remembered, Paul looked at his empty fingers. The parchment had slipped out of his hands and fallen to the floor. In his mind he knew that the ring was the only thing that had the power to save him.

Pirates: Chapter 29

The Family Plot

As Kate prepared herself for the funeral her mind raced through all of the years that they had spent hiding and she tried not to cry. She thought about the day they left the plantation -- how gently Paul had carried their sleeping children to the carriage and how he had kissed each one as he placed them inside. Kate had ridden on top with Paul and for more than an hour, as he drove, he tried to explain the best he could what had taken place. He showed her the ring and its inscription.

Kate had, of course, heard stories about The Ring of Hope, and she listened as Paul explained about his father and how he had come to wear it. She tried to accept that she and the kids needed to hide to be safe, but she really didn't understand why Paul couldn't just throw the ring away. Mostly she tried to come to terms with the idea of living apart. Kate understood that Paul had to find the man behind the attack, but she didn't have to like it. The ring was a strange concept, but she knew from what had happened that night -- from that strange, hazy lack of memory that nagged at her -- that it was the only explanation.

Paul tried hiding them in several different places during the year that followed, but, in their own world, none of them ever felt safe. However, Paul, unlike previous owners of the ring, continued to see the ring as a source of hope, and he discovered many things about it that no one else had. With each discovery came more hope and then, one day, Paul came upon the ability to move himself in time. One second he would be in the world that he had always known, and the next he found himself in a world unlike any he had ever seen. It was the same in some ways, but it was much more modern and civilized. There were things in this world that he had never seen before, and opportunities he never could have imagined.

Paul spent months exploring its possibilities before he presented the idea to Kate. The only downside, at first, was that they would be able to bring only the clothes they were wearing; you couldn't carry anything while you passed through time. But, with a little trial and error, Paul soon found that if he buried something in the old world, he could uncover it in the new one -- he just had to find the same location. Then, to his great surprise, he learned that his buried treasures were worth more money in the new world than he could have ever dreamed of. Some people would refer to them as antiques, and he was told that museums and private collectors would pay enormous amounts of money for what they referred to as artifacts from a time gone by.

After careful consideration, Paul came to Kate one night with a plan. He explained to her what he had seen and said that he believed she could live freely with the children in this new world without worry. It was a hard decision for Kate, but she yearned to be someplace where they would be safe again. She decided that she and the children would go and she would learn the ways of this strange new world. Her only sadness was that Paul would not stay with them. He explained that he still needed to follow his quest and find the man behind the attack so that one day they could all return to their home together.

Kate finished combing her hair, pulling it back off her face and securing it to the back of her head with a silver clip. At forty years old, Kate's auburn hair had not a single strand of gray and her skin was wrinkle free, making her look at least ten years younger than she was.

Time had been kind to Kate, and the modern world fit her like a glove. She had quickly fallen in love with her new surroundings and knew if she had ever had to make a choice that she would not return to the ways of old. She enjoyed the simple conveniences -- things like lights, flushing toilets, running water and being able to toss everyone's clothes into a machine for washing. It was all amazing (although she often joked that it would be a perfect life only if someone could come up with something to fold and put away the laundry, too).

Kate was putting the final touches on her lips when she was beckoned out of her thoughts.

"Mom, are you almost ready? We have to go," Peter called out.

"I will be down in a minute," she answered.

Kate didn't really like makeup, but she wouldn't leave the house without lipstick and a little mascara on her eyelashes. She looked into the mirror and smiled as she thought about Peter. Although she had grown fond of this new life, she also was tired of living with the lies and was so happy that the kids finally knew the truth about their father. The three years Peter had spent with the man he knew as Captain Paul were fun for him, and they would provide Peter with happy memories that he would cherish forever.

Kate sat in church with Peter on one side and Belle on the other, listening as the priest talked about life and the ones who are left behind at the end of it. She knew he was talking about life and death and the hereafter, but Kate was thinking about what he was saying as it applied to her own life. The one she left behind she could hardly remember now, and the new one, though it had become a place they could call home, made her leave someone behind. The one to come, she hoped, was one lived as a family, a family that she prayed would one day include Paul. The years had been lonely at times, with Paul coming and going, but the kids had given her a purpose. The hardest part of it all was the ever-present fear that one day Paul would just not return and she wouldn't know what had happened to him. That was the reason she first agreed to allow Peter to be a part of Paul's world.

Kate watched as the six pallbearers slid the coffin into the back of the hearse and shut the door. On the drive to the cemetery Kate again sat in the middle of her two children, holding their hands tightly, and tried to clear her head. The procession of cars slowed down as the lead car pulled into Rolling Hills Cemetery. It was a peaceful place and Kate found herself thinking that it wasn't too morbid if you didn't think about it too much.

As the mourners gathered at the grave site, Kate looked at the headstone and admired the etching around the edges. The names of Paul's parents, having been carved years ago, were a little more worn than Charles's,

251

Paul's and Kate's, which were all newly engraved. Looking at her own name on a grave marker made her cringe, but at least only her birth date was next to it. "No date of death yet," she thought thankfully. But because it was a family plot, she knew that one day she would join them here.

Peter was also looking at the stone and thinking about his ancestry. As he looked at the name Charles Martin Delham, he couldn't help but wonder what would drive a man to do what he did.

"Mom," Peter said softly.

"What Peter?"

"Why did dad want Uncle Charles brought back here? He did nothing but hurt people."

"Despite the choices Charles made in his adult life, your father and his brother had good times growing up together and that is what he wanted to remember. That is also what he wants us to keep in mind. In the end your father chose to forgive him, Peter, and that is what we must do, too."

"Forgive him?" asked Peter.

"Yes," Kate replied, though she knew that was asking a lot.

"I will try, Mom, but I can't make any promises."

"That is all you can do, Peter."

When the funeral ended, everyone threw a flower onto the grave, returned back to their vehicles and left the cemetery. A while later, Monk heard a car pull into the driveway and ran to the window to see who it was. Peter was back and it was a lot earlier than he expected. When Peter walked into the bedroom, Monk was excited to see him.

"What are you doing back so soon?" Monk asked.

"We're not staying. We just stopped for a few minutes because Mom forgot something, and she said I could change out of this monkey suit before we go to the luncheon."

"Monkey suit?" asked Monk. "Is that an attempt at humor, because you don't look anything like a monkey."

Peter sighed. He might have laughed under different circumstances, but not today. "It's just something they call a . . . you know, Monk, that's what you can do while I'm gone. Find out why they call it that."

"No thanks, I'm not that interested. Besides, I am reading your story," Monk said excitedly.

"You're reading it again? How many times is that now?"

"Five! It is really good, but I am still disappointed that you left me out of the end of the story. I think Miss Bell is going to be very disappointed."

"Monk, I just told the story the way it happened and, as I remember it, you spent the whole time in that palm tree."

"Hey!" Monk said, clearly offended. "My job was one of the most important ones in the whole mission."

"Monk, I am not denying that your role was important, but after your signal there was no way to tie you in and make it interesting," Peter explained.

"Well, you could have taken me out of the tree and had me doing battle with that Mario guy, or anyone, really . . ."

"Monk, that isn't what happened."

"The reader doesn't know that. All I am saying is that you could make a few small adjustments, ones that wouldn't change the outcome, and give your readers what they want."

"And, remind me again, what do they want?" Peter asked, smiling, as he changed into khakis and a polo shirt.

"Me, Peter! I am a pivotal part of your story and I totally disappear at the end." Monk was pouting.

"Peter, are you ready to go yet?" yelled Kate from downstairs. "There are guests waiting for us. Let's go."

"I'm coming, Mom. I just have to put on my shoes," Peter yelled down the stairs. "I have to go, Monk. Enjoy the story."

"Peter, can I ask you a favor?"

"It depends what it is. What is it?"

"Just think about what I said, okay? It will really

make the story better."

Peter rolled his eyes and smiled. "I will think about it, but don't get your hopes up."

"Peter, that is all I am asking. Thanks."

"You're welcome," Peter said as he walked out of his room.

Peter came down the steps two at a time. His mom was standing by the front door.

"It's about time. What were you doing up there?" she asked.

"It was Monk. He doesn't like that he isn't in the end of the story I wrote for school and he wants me to change it."

"So what did you tell him?"

"I told him that I would think about it."

Kate nodded. "That's fair."

"I thought so," Peter said, proud of himself. "And Mom?"

"What?"

"You know you don't have any lipstick on."

Kate wrinkled her nose and frowned. "All that time waiting for you and I totally forgot to refresh. I'll be right back." She turned to go up the stairs, then stopped, turning back around. "Peter, give this to your father and tell him to put it on. He left it on the dresser. I will be right out."

Kate handed Peter a gold band and disappeared up the

steps. Peter walked out of the house and hopped into the backseat of his dad's car. Paul turned his head to look at his son as he got in and realized that his brother was right -- Peter did resemble his mother.

Peter held out his hand. "Dad, Mom found this on your dresser," he said, holding up the ring. "She told me to tell you to put it on."

"I bet she did," Paul said laughing. As he reached to take the ring, he noticed that Peter was looking at the inscription. "What is it, Peter?"

"Isn't this the ring you told us about, The Ring of Hope?" Peter asked.

"Yes, it is."

"But you told Uncle Charles that Matais took the ring."

"Yes, I did, but I lied. Matais did take a ring, but not the real one. Matais took a ring that my mother had specially made for my brother. It was an exact duplicate of my ring, including the inscription on it."

"That's what he was talking about on the ship," Peter remarked.

"You heard that, did you?"

"Yes, I heard everything, except what was said after I shut the door."

"Peter, the truth is, my mother didn't think Charles could handle the power that went with this ring and she didn't want him to have it. I thought she was wrong. My father wanted him to have it and, at the time, I thought that she should have done what my father requested."

"But she was right."

"As it turns out, she was. But in doing the right thing she lost a child."

"What do you mean, Dad?"

"Your uncle was so angry over the rings that he stopped talking to both of us. I always hoped that one day he would come to his senses, and I promised myself that I would do the right thing and give him the ring."

"It's a good thing you didn't!" Peter exclaimed.

"I guess," Paul said, sounding unsure. "Who knows how things would have turned out if she had just given him the ring to begin with."

"Why did you keep both rings?"

"I'll be honest, I was a little selfish. I liked the ring and I wanted one, so if some day I gave Charles the real one, I figured at least I would still have one to wear. It didn't matter to me if it wasn't the real thing."

"But when he wouldn't talk to you for so long, why did you still keep it? I think that I would have gotten rid of it a long time ago."

"He was my brother, Peter. He was my family and I couldn't let him go that easily. I never stopped hoping that some day he would change his mind, so I kept the ring locked in a desk drawer. Then when Captain Warner came gunning for me, I decided that it was time to use it

257

to my advantage. If Warner wanted The Ring of Hope, he certainly wasn't going to get the real one if I could help it, so the moment I found out about Matais, I switched rings. I never would have let him take the real one so easily."

"But Dad! Whether or not the ring was the real one, he could have killed you!"

"He thought I was either already dead or soon to be, Peter, so I didn't think he would do anything."

"That was a scary chance to take." Peter frowned at Paul disapprovingly.

"It was a little, but you know what?"

"What?"

"It was worth the chance. I wanted us all back together as a family and the only way that was going to happen was if someone else claimed the ring. As sure as the sun is shining right now, I am sure that Matais has spent the last week bragging to everyone he knows how he stole The Ring of Hope away from Captain Paul."

"But that's stupid. If he does that, people will try to take it from him."

"Unfortunately, that is the price of owning the ring and letting people know that you have it. My father never told a soul he had this ring, not even my Mother, and he lived a life that was free from this torment. We must do the same thing. It must always remain a secret, Peter. I had always kept the ring a secret, but Charles knew about it. I never would have imagined that he would come after it the way that he did, but, well . . . now Matais has removed the burden from our shoulders, leaving us free to go anywhere we want and feel safe."

"Anywhere?" Peter's eyes lit up, thinking of the possibilities.

"Anywhere that has running water and a toilet that flushes," Paul said, laughing, as Kate climbed into the car.

"What was that about toilets that flush?" asked Kate, smiling.

"Oh, I was just telling Peter about the ring being our family secret and how we can go anywhere as long as they have indoor plumbing."

"Room service would be nice, too," chimed in Nic from the backseat. Everyone started laughing.

"Belle Nicole Delham, you have been so quiet today that I almost forgot you were with us," Kate commented.

"I've just been thinking, Mom."

"About what, honey," Paul asked.

Nic looked sadly at her father. "Dad, are we ever going back?"

"Nic, my love, you were the best lookout a captain could ever have asked for, and the fact that Peter never figured out it was you always amused me," Paul said teasingly .

"Dad, she was dressed like a boy and she never left the lookout! How was I supposed to know it was her, and, anyway, she didn't recognize me, either," Peter protested.

"Peter, I was only kidding. There are a lot of things that The Ring of Hope can do to keep us safe, and one of them is to make people see things differently than what is real. That is why you and Nic both saw me as Captain Paul and not as Dad. If anyone had known that I was your father they could have used you to get to me."

Impatiently, Nic cut in. "Dad, you didn't answer me. Are we ever going back?"

Paul took a deep breath before answering. He turned around fully in the driver's seat to look at his children. "Both of you have seen what that world is like -- at the best of times it is dangerous. I only survived those poisoned letters because of the ring, and even if no one there thinks I have it anymore, there is no guarantee that we can fend off every pirate that wants to take something from us. We have done all that we need to do there for right now and, if the ring continues to allow it, we are going to stay right here."

Nic pouted. "I miss the sea and the ship, Dad."

"Me too," Peter added, sounding disappointed.

"Well . . . how about I buy us a big sail boat?" Paul offered.

"And a beach house?" asked Peter, his eyebrows

raised, smiling.

Kate tilted her head and looked at Paul. "Actually, a beach house does sound nice, Paul," she piped in.

Nic giggled. "Look, Dad, we all agree! How often does *that* happen? And a beach house would be a great place to hide. No one would ever look for us there." Nic crossed her fingers, hoping that her dad said yes.

Paul looked around at the faces of his family.

"What do you say, Paul?" Kate asked.

Paul laughed. "I don't know why you all think you have to work so hard to convince me. I love the beach and I am already losing my tan."

Kate laughed, and the kids started to cheer.

As Paul turned the key in the ignition, he realized he hadn't put the ring back on yet. He reached back, took it from Peter's hand and slipped it on his finger, then started to back out of the driveway. Suddenly he stopped the car and everyone turned to look at him.

"Paul, what is it? Why did you stop like that?" Kate asked.

"This is a day about family and it just feels wrong that Monk is sitting in the house by himself. Peter, go up and get him. Tell him that I want him to come with us."

"Okay, Dad." Peter smiled. "He's going to like this!" Peter jumped out of the car and ran up the front steps, into the house.

Less than a minute later, Peter and Monk came running back out and got in the car. Paul caught a glimpse of Nic as he looked in the rearview mirror to back out, again, and then he glanced back at Peter and Monk. He reached over and took Kate's hand. Paul had not felt this hopeful in a very long time. He knew how lucky he was and he couldn't ask for anything else on Earth -- but, he would keep the ring, just in case.

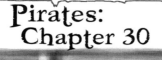

Pirates: Chapter 30

Footsteps in the Dark

Paul had tucked both of the kids into bed with hugs and kisses and now stood in the doorway of the kitchen watching Kate put the dishes away. He was thinking back on that night many years ago, at the orchard, when he had almost lost his family. The kids were toddlers then and he couldn't help but feel a little remorseful that his decision had caused him to lose so much time with them. But tonight he had them back for good. He would go to bed with his wife and kids safely under his roof and, for the first time in years, he felt like a rich man again.

Kate turned and saw Paul looking at her. She smiled.

She was so thankful that he was home and there would be no more running. Paul walked over to her without saying a word, took her in his arms and hugged her tight. She was warm, comforting and her hair smelled lightly of coconut, which made him smile. Kate had always given him hope -- he would have never made it through these past years without her in his heart and dreams -- but now life was the way it should be, he thought.

*   *   *

The sound of footsteps echoed in the night as the man walked down the gravel path that lead to the front of the house. He knew he was just a shadow in the dark from this distance so he stopped for a second to see what could be seen through the windows. There was a light on in the living room and he could barely make out the sound of a man and a woman talking. He crept closer and then tiptoed up the steps to the front door. As he took his last step before reaching the door, a loose board in the flooring squeaked. His body tightened as he heard it and he stopped. He clenched his jaw as he stood there, motionless, for a minute, and then he went back to business. He gently turned the doorknob, hoping that the door would open, but it turned only slightly. The door was locked.

*   *   *

Paul told Kate that he would be right up to bed -- he wanted to shut the windows in the living room just in case it rained. As Paul closed the last of the windows and flipped the latch to lock it, he heard a sound on the front porch. He looked out the window but couldn't see anything in the darkness. Then Paul heard the sound again, but this time it sounded like it was near the front door. Paul grabbed the iron fireplace poker from its stand and walked quietly through the living room and foyer to the front door. As he stood there, he heard it again.

*   *   *

With the front door locked, the man walked slowly across the porch and climbed over the railing. He walked through the grass to the back door, hoping for better luck. When he twisted the knob, the door swung open and he stepped noiselessly into the mud room. He walked to the entrance of the kitchen and looked around -- there was no one in sight, but he could tell they were close by. He removed the leather satchel that hung from his shoulder to pull out its contents. When he had the package firmly in hand he gingerly removed it from the bag and returned the satchel to his shoulder.

*   *   *

Paul stood at the door with the fire poker and flipped the switch to the porch light. "Shoot! It must need a new bulb," Paul said to himself when nothing happened. Paul's heart began to race as he turned the dead bolt and heard it click. He raised the poker up in the air, prepared to strike, then pulled the door open wide. Suddenly Tilly leapt from the darkness, ran through Paul's legs and into the house. Paul was so startled that he started to swing the poker but he stopped himself just in time.

"Tilly, you scared me!" Paul yelled. Then Paul started to laugh. He was amused with himself and feeling foolish since here he was, standing on his front porch in his boxer shorts, with a fireplace poker, battling Nic's cute orange tabby. He turned around in time to watch the cat's backside trot down the hallway in victory and disappear into the kitchen. Paul closed the door and secured the lock before returning the poker to the living room. He started to turn to go upstairs when the photographs on the mantle caught his attention. He smiled and reached for his favorite.

*　　　*　　　*

The man walked through the shadows of the dark kitchen trying not to make a sound, heading towards the room with the light. Stopping just shy of the doorway, he stretched to peek his head in enough to see who was in there. He pulled back with a smile on his face and looked down at the package in his hand. He realized that this was long overdue and the fact that it was gong to be a surprise was going to make it that much more enjoyable.

As he stepped into the living room, the light reflected off of the silver skulls on his boots and he was seen. Marcus started to put his finger to his lips to signal to his father to stay quiet, when his mouth dropped open in shock, realizing that *it was his father* standing there. Before he could speak, his mother, who had been sitting with her back to him, saw that Dalti was looking intently at something and turned to look. When she saw her son standing there, her heart skipped and she put her hand over her mouth to try to stop herself from crying. Marcus, still in shock over the sight of his father, reached out the hand that held the package and said, "Happy birthday, Mom." Now she couldn't help herself; the tears just came. Dalti had survived the haunted ravine, finally finding his way out, and now her son, too, had returned home! It was too much for her to handle in one day and she just let herself cry with relief.

*   *   *

Paul was still in the living room when he heard someone come into the room. As he turned towards the doorway, they locked eyes. Paul set the frame back onto the mantle and blew out the two candles that were lit next to it while not breaking eye contact. Monk stared back as he climbed onto the couch.

267

"Monk, what are you doing awake?" Paul asked.

"I needed to talk to you, Mr. Paul."

"Mr. Paul?" said Paul, looking somewhat confused. "I haven't heard anyone call me that in a long time." Just as Paul was saying this, a white cloudy haze formed around Monk. "Monk?" said Paul, alarmed, as he watched the monkey they all knew so well disappear into the mist. A second later, in Monk's place stood Tret. He had the same eerie presence he did that day they spoke in the barn. "Tret? It can't be."

"It's nice to see you, Mr. Paul."

Paul was staring at his old stable hand in complete disbelief. "Tret, you're Monk?"

"No, not really, Mr. Paul. You could say that I have been guiding him just a little," Tret said, smiling.

"Why didn't you tell me?"

"Because I couldn't . . . and it wasn't something that you needed to know, anyway. I was sent to help Monk get familiar with the world. He was unaware of many things and needed guidance."

Paul laughed and said, "I would *say* he needed guidance. He was a stuffed animal, a toy!"

"You asked the ring for someone to watch over your family and it sent you Monk."

"I assumed that was why Monk came along. It isn't often that one sees a stuffed animal come to life."

"At one time he was a stuffed animal, but have no

doubts, Monk is real. To Peter, Monk has always been real. You wished for someone to watch over your family while you were gone and Monk was the perfect choice. He was here and Peter loved him so much that it never seemed strange to him that he truly became a live monkey. But, like you said, Monk had been a stuffed toy and couldn't think for himself. That is why I was asked to help him."

"So, then, you *are* Monk." Paul felt like their conversation was going in circles, but Tret continued to explain,

"At first I was a big part of what helped Monk process his thoughts. But then he didn't need my help anymore so, no, I'm not Monk."

Paul was confused. "What changed? Why didn't he need help anymore?"

"Do you remember the day you left the magic boots for Peter to find?"

"Of course I do."

"Well, on that day, when Peter entered the old world -- Captain Paul's world -- Monk went with him. But Monk could not be part of that world as a toy so he became real. He was kind of like the wooden boy in that story Peter used to read to Monk everyday, Pinokey Noise. Only Monk became real by the power of the ring, not by a fairy granting a wish."

"You mean Pinocchio," Paul said, smiling, as he

remembered how much Peter loved that story.

"Yes, that's the one."

"Okay, Tret, so Monk is now completely real and only *guided* by you instead of having his thoughts processed by you. What is the importance of this distinction? Why are you telling me this?"

"I'm telling you this now because I'm leaving and you needed to know that, once I'm gone, Monk will be on his own."

Paul was still not clear on what any of this meant, and now he was concerned about what was going to happen to Monk. "What does that mean, Tret? What will happen to Monk? Monk is part of our family."

"Nothing will happen to him, Mr. Paul. Monk is smart and has been thinking and making decisions for himself for some time now. I only stayed this long as a precaution."

"So Monk will continue to watch over our family?"

"Yes, sir."

"So if nothing is changing, why are you really here, Tret? If Monk is going to be the same after you leave, there must be another reason why you came."

"Mr. Paul, before you found out about Charles you were fearful, and because of this fear you were alert to the dangers that your situation presented. Now you are feeling at ease and you've let your guard down."

"So what are you telling me, that we still are not

safe?" This very idea made Paul's heart and head start to race.

"No, Mr. Paul. What I mean to tell you is that it's important to keep your eyes open and your guard up. Be well, Mr. Paul."

Panic was setting in. "For what? What do I need to keep my guard up for? What should I . . . "

Paul's voice trailed off because, before he could finish his thought, the white haze again appeared and Tret vanished, leaving Monk soundly sleeping in the corner of the couch. The words "keep your eyes open and your guard up" were throbbing in his head. He wanted to know what Tret meant by this. Are they really still in danger? Paul thought back to the day that he spoke to Tret in the barn and how Tret had told him that the pirates would return. He realized that this warning was different, less urgent, and started to relax slightly. But he also knew that he shouldn't ignore what Tret had told him and he promised himself that he would be watchful for his family's safety.

Paul's thoughts were diverted by the sounds of squeaking floorboards and shuffling feet. He heard a bang in the kitchen, like someone bumped into one of the chairs at the dining table. He started to reach for the fireplace poker once again when he spotted a pair of the deepest blue eyes in the flicker of the firelight. Paul immediately smiled. Those beautiful eyes -- blue like

271

the ocean, peaceful and kind -- looked very sleepy at the moment.

"Nic, are you awake?" Paul said softly as he walked towards his daughter, but Nic didn't answer. She just stood still and stared at Paul. Paul knelt down in front of her and repeated himself, "Nic, are you awake?"

Paul had to stifle a laugh at her reaction. Nic closed her eyes and puckered up her lips like a fish, kissing the air in front of Paul. He had forgotten that his daughter was a sleepwalker. She had been doing this since she learned to walk and the fish kisses were a telltale sign that she was indeed sleeping. Paul put his hand on Nic's back to try to guide her back to bed and couldn't stop himself from laughing as she continued to blow kisses as they walked.

"Paul, I thought that you were coming to bed an hour ago," Kate called softly from the top of the stairs.

"I'm coming now," Paul said, still laughing.

"You need to be a little quieter, you're going to wake the kids! What in the world is so funny, anyway?"

"Nic is sleepwalking," Paul said with amusement as he led Nic into the foyer from the living room.

"Ohhh. She's doing the guppy lips, isn't she?" Kate asked knowingly, then quickly ran down the steps so she could see.

When Kate got to the bottom, Paul walked back in front of Nic and asked again, "Nic, are you awake?"

Paul and Kate were both laughing as Nic again did her puckered up fish kisses response.

Kate, giggling like a little girl, said, "Paul, you have to stop, that's not nice."

"You should get the video camera and tape this," was his response.

"No, we should not. She would be so angry if we did that."

Paul persisted. "But Kate, she won't do this forever and one day we will forget she ever did it. We should have it on video."

"If you need help remembering, I promise I will remind you, but I am not letting you put it on video." Paul started to search for the camera. "Please, don't," Kate begged. "It will only embarrass her. Let's just put her to bed."

Paul sighed. "She is just so darn cute when she does that." He paused for a second, got a mischievous look on his face, then said, "Nic, are you awake?"

Kate and Paul looked at each other and smiled, then turned to watch Nic one last time doing her guppy lips. They were enjoying this moment together, knowing full well that Nic wouldn't continue sleepwalking like this forever. Then Paul bent down and scooped Nic up into his arms to carry her upstairs. Kate followed them up the steps and they both tucked her back into bed. When they turned to leave the room, Paul noticed a piece of paper leaning up against the flowered piggy bank on Nic's dresser. It said "Daddy" across the front. As Paul took a step towards the note, Kate smiled and said,

"Read it. She wanted you to find it."

Paul picked up the paper and opened it. The inside was decorated with all kinds of doodles and pictures that Nic had drawn, and in the middle, in her not-too-long-ago mastered cursive writing, it read:

I love you Daddy! Welcome home!

As Paul read the note, both he and Kate saw his ring start to glow brightly in the darkness, but it was Kate's gold wedding band that caught them both by surprise -- it shimmered and shined as brightly as his! She quickly removed the ring from her finger to examine it and was stunned and awed by her discovery. An inscription had mysteriously appeared on the inside of her band, and it was a perfect match to Paul's.

"To all that need hope"

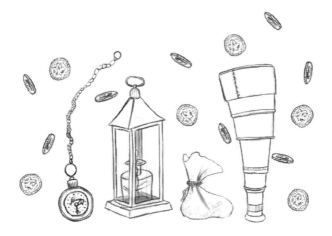

Daryl Cobb lives in New Jersey with his family, not far from his childhood hometown. Daryl's writing began in college as a Theatre Arts major at Virginia Commonwealth University. He found a freshman writing class  inspiring and, combined with his love for music and the guitar, he discovered a passion for songwriting. This talent would motivate him for years to come and the rhythm he created with his music also found its way into the bedtime stories he later created for his children. Through the years his son and daughter have inspired much of his work, including "Boy on the Hill", "Daniel Dinosaur" and "Daddy Did I Ever Say? I Love You, Love You, Every Day".

When Daryl isn't writing or plucking on his guitar he is visiting schools promoting literacy with his interactive educational assemblies. Daryl is one of New Jersey's premier educational performers whose use of performance arts to teach and entertain has educators and assembly coordinators everywhere consistently calling his school programs "the best of the best." These performance programs teach children about the writing and creative processes and allow Daryl to do what he feels is most important -- inspire children to read and write.

Made in the USA
Charleston, SC
28 January 2012